Critical acclaim for
AWFUL END
Book One of the Eddie Dickens Trilogy

'[A] scrumptious cross between Dickens and Monty
Python . . . You can look at this book as an examination
of: 1) the absurdities of the English language; 2) the
absurdities of the 19th-century novel; 3) the absurdities of
the way the English treat their kids; 4) the absurdities of
the absurd. A child will enjoy its daftness at 10, will get
the references at 14, and will know that it is all true at 18
. . . Brilliant.'
LYN GARDNER, *Guardian*

' . . . sophisticated . . . extremely silly . . . wonderful
. . . ridiculing literary conventions and turning
nonsense into a fine art.'
DINAH HALL, *Sunday Telegraph*

'It would be a sad spirit that didn't find
this book hilarious.'
LUCY JAMES, *Financial Times*

'In this surreal world, language is never what it
appears . . . It's daft but entirely engaging.'
HILARY MACASKILL, *Independent*

'Ardagh has a brilliantly witty style of writing . . .
A future classic and no mistake.'
Crowdsurfer.com

'A delicious slice of the ridiculous. A real find.'
TARA STEPHENSON, *Bookseller*

Dreadful Acts

Over two metres tall, with a bushy beard, Philip Ardagh is not only very large and very hairy but has also written over fifty children's books for all ages. *Dreadful Acts* is the second book in the Eddie Dickens Trilogy, which began with the critically acclaimed *Awful End*.

Currently living as a full-time writer, with a wife and two cats in a seaside town somewhere in England, he has been – amongst other things – an advertising copywriter, a hospital cleaner, a (highly unqualified) librarian, and a reader for the blind.

'One of my favourite comic characters is back in the second part of his hilarious history . . . and the result is equally delicious, and ridiculous.'
TARA STEPHENSON, *Bookseller*

by the same author
published by Faber & Faber

Fiction

Awful End
Book One of the Eddie Dickens Trilogy

The Fall of Fergal
Book One of the Unlikely Exploits Series

Non-fiction

The Hieroglyphs Handbook
Teach Yourself Ancient Egyptian

The Archaeologist's Handbook
The Insider's Guide to Digging Up the Past

Did Dinosaurs Snore?
100$^1/_2$ Questions about Dinosaurs Answered

Why Are Castles Castle-Shaped?
100$^1/_2$ Questions about Castles Answered

PHILIP ARDAGH

Dreadful
Acts

Book Two of the Eddie Dickens Trilogy

illustrated by David Roberts

faber and faber

First published in 2001
by Faber and Faber Limited
3 Queen Square, London WC1N 3AU

Typeset by Faber and Faber Limited
Printed in England by Mackays of Chatham plc, Chatham, Kent

A CIP record for this book
is available from the British Library

ISBN 0-571-20947-5

4 6 8 10 9 7 5 3

A Message from the Author

Because he likes you

*D*readful Acts is the sequel to *Awful End*, in which Eddie Dickens (and a number of other characters who lurk within these pages) were first let loose on the reading public. You don't have to have read *Awful End* for this book to make sense, it's a story in its own right . . . and I'm not sure that *Awful End* made a great deal of sense, anyway. If you enjoy this book, please be sure to tell all your friends about it. If you hate it, please be sure to keep your ill-informed opinions to yourself.

Thank you

PHILIP ARDAGH

England
2001

For everyone who has helped to make *Awful End* the success it is.

Thank you.
You know who you are.

Contents

Episode 1

Here We Go Again

In which a hssss becomes a BOOOOM!

Eddie Dickens woke up with a shock. An electric eel had just landed on him from the top pocket of his great uncle's overcoat. And one thing that can be guaranteed to be shocking is electricity.

Eddie sat up. 'What's happening, Mad Uncle Jack?' he asked, for that was the name he called the thinnest of thin gentleman – with the beakiest of beaky noses – who was leaning over his bed.

'Come quickly, boy!' his great-uncle instructed, his top hat brushing against the gas tap of the lamp on the wall. The eel might have had electricity, but this house – Awful End – didn't.

Eddie didn't need to be asked twice. The quickest way to escape the eel was to leap from his bed, so leap from his bed he did.

Eddie and his parents lived at Awful End with his great-uncle and great-aunt (Mad Aunt Maud). If you want to find out how they all came to live together, following a series of awfully exciting adventures – though I say so myself – you'll have to read the first book in this trilogy, called (surprise, surprise) *Awful End*.

Now where were we? Oh yes: an electric eel in the bed, Eddie Dickens out of the bed, and Mad Uncle Jack's top hat brushing against the gas tap . . . What's that hissing noise? Do you think it's important? Do you think it's part of the plot?

Hsssssssssssssssssssssssssssssssssssssssssssssssssss.

Mad Uncle Jack snatched up the escaped eel, seemingly unconcerned as the current of electricity passed through his hand and up his arm as he popped it back in his pocket. This rather strange gentleman used dried fish (and eels) to pay his bills but, for some reason we're bound to discover later, this eel was still alive and slipping. (I can't really say 'alive and *kicking*' now, can I? Eels – electric or otherwise – don't have legs.)

Eddie glanced at the clock on the wall. It said six o'clock in the morning.

'Six o'clock in the morning,' said the clock – an old joke, but not bad for a clock.

Why was Mad Uncle Jack getting him up so

2

early, Eddie wondered? It must be important. Then again, perhaps not. After all, his great-uncle was completely mad. Stifling a yawn, Eddie pulled on his clothes.

'Hurry!' said Mad Uncle Jack through gritted teeth. He didn't have a gritted pair of his own, so he always carried a pre-gritted pair about his person for just such an occasion. He kept these in a side pocket of his coat rather than in a top pocket. This was why the electric eel, rather than the pair of pre-gritted teeth, had fallen onto his great nephew.

Out on the landing, the early light of dawn filtered through the large picture window. A picture window is a big window, usually with a large enough area of glass to permit one to see a view as pretty as a picture. (Not to be confused with a picture *of a* window, which is – er – a picture *of a* window.)

The view from this window was of Mad Uncle Jack's tree house, built entirely of dried fish, and covered in creosote. The creosote not only protected the tree house from bad weather, but also from the neighbourhood cats (who loved the smell and taste of dried fish but who hated the smell and taste of creosote). Some might think the tree house pretty in the pinky early-morning light. There was something quite *salmony* about it. That's the word: salmony.

Still half asleep – which, if my maths serves me correctly, means that he must also have been half awake – Eddie Dickens followed Mad Uncle Jack down the front stairs. He lost his footing a couple of times but managed to remain upright and stumble on.

The heavy velvet curtains were closed in the hallway and it was pitch-black. Pitch is a kind of gooey tar which is very, very black, so pitch-black is a way of saying 'very, very black' using fewer letters . . . so long as you don't then have to explain what 'pitch' is, as I've just done.

Mad Uncle Jack found the front door by walking into it. The advantage of having the beakiest of beaky noses was that it reached the door way in front of the rest of him, so he managed to limit his injuries.

'Oooof!' he said, which is the universal noise a person makes when walking into a door, unless he or she stubs a toe, that is. The universal noise for stubbing a toe is 'Arrrgh!!!' (but you can choose the number of exclamation marks that best suits).

'Are you all right?' asked Eddie, blinded moments later as his great-uncle threw the door open wide, letting in the morning sunshine.

'There's no time to lose, boy,' said Mad Uncle Jack, a trickle of blood running from his beak– nose, I mean *nose*.

The picture window on the landing looked out onto his tree house at the back of the building. The front door opened onto the *front* – the clue is in the name – and there, right in the middle of the huge sweep of gravel driveway, was a hearse.

A hearse served the same purpose then as a hearse serves today. It was for transporting dead bodies in coffins from A to B (assuming that you *wanted* the coffin taken from A to B – it might be taken from A to Z if you asked very nicely). The difference is that hearses today are sleek black motor cars, whereas motor cars hadn't been invented in Eddie Dickens's day. For that reason, hearses were often glass-sided carriages pulled – or 'drawn', as horsy folk would say – by a pair of black horses with plumes of black feathers. The driver of a hearse would be dressed in black too . . . only this hearse didn't appear to have a driver and the coffin was half in and half out of the back.

The horses appeared nervous, skittish even (whatever that may mean), and they were shuffling their hooves around uneasily. Their flesh looked sweaty and their eyes were wide.

Mad Uncle Jack was already scrunching across the gravel. Eddie ran to keep up. 'W-What's happening?' he gasped. 'Who . . . who's died?'

'Your parents are asleep upstairs and Mad Aunt Maud is safely tucked up in Marjorie,' Mad Uncle Jack reassured him. Marjorie was a cow-shaped carnival float that Eddie's great-aunt lived inside in the gardens of Awful End. If you don't know why, I wouldn't let it bother you. It won't really lessen your reading enjoyment. 'I was awoken by the sound of frightened horses and this is what I found . . . a riderless hearse.'

'And this is what you got me up to see?' asked Eddie, nervously. If these pitch-black – yes, that word 'pitch' again – horses bolted, the coffin was bound to fall to the driveway and smash open . . . and who knew what or *who* might spill out onto the ground.

'Indeed. I do not want your great-aunt troubled by such a sight. She is a sensitive creature. And your parents need their sleep with the busy day that lies ahead. I feel confident that, with your experience of training horses, we'll soon have this carriage off the premises.'

'But I've never trained horses,' Eddie Dickens explained, patiently. Living with Mad Uncle Jack and Mad Aunt Maud, you had to be patient.

'So you've lied to me all these years then, have you, Edmund?' said his great-uncle sternly. 'Next you'll be telling me that you never fought along-side Colonel Marley at the Fall of St Geobad.'

'I think you're confusing me with someone else,' Eddie protested. 'I'm only thirteen. Well, almost.'

Mad Uncle Jack frowned. 'You've never trained horses?'

Eddie shook his head.

'And you never fought alongside Colonel Marley at the Fall of St Geobad?'

'No, sir,' said Eddie. 'I don't even know what the Fall of St Geobad is.'

'Me neither,' said Mad Uncle Jack, 'and there'd be no point in asking you now.'

'Do you think it might have been a waterfall?' Eddie suggested, helpfully.

'St Geobad seems a ridiculous name for a waterfall to me, boy. Preposterous! I've often wondered whether St Geobad was a church.'

'A church that fell down?' Eddie mused. 'But

why would Colonel Marley be fighting by a falling-down church?'

'A point well made! Well made, sir!' said his great-uncle. 'Perhaps it means "fall" as in "autumn".'

One of the horses at the front of the hearse snorted, causing steam to rise from its nostrils and the reader to remember the hearse, which was in serious danger of being forgotten because Uncle Jack – *Mad* Uncle Jack, that is – and Eddie Dickens were getting sidetracked.

'Well, you're here now, boy,' said Mad Uncle Jack, 'so what I want you to do is to calm the horses whilst I go to the back of the hearse and push the coffin back inside.'

Eddie would have preferred it if his great-uncle had done the calming-of-the-horses and he'd gone round to the back of the hearse. He knew from books he'd read – such as *Life After Being Kicked* and *Horsy Horrors*, for starters – that nervous horses were inclined to kick out at people who turned up uninvited to try to calm them down . . . but, then again, Mad Uncle Jack was a lot stronger than he was. He'd be able to slide the coffin back inside much more easily.

'G-G-Good horses . . . nice horses . . .' said Eddie in the kind of voice some people use when they're cooing over a baby in a pram, saying 'Doesn't he have his mother's eyes?' (If a baby *really* had his mother's eyes, she'd be screaming her head off and calling for child psychologist, police and ambulance and trying to get the eyes back off him.)

He took a step forward. *Scrunch.*

Both horses fixed their wide eyes on his. They reminded Eddie of the glass eyes on Mad Aunt Maud's stuffed stoat, Malcolm.

He took another step forward. *Scrunch.*

The horses' eyes looked even more wild . . . even more crazy, if that was possible. Forget Malcolm. They reminded Eddie of Even Madder Aunt Maud herself, now.

Scrunch.

One of the horses whinnied.

Eddie dug his hand inside the pockets of his

trousers. In one was a carrot and in the other a fistful of sugar lumps. What a lucky break! What were the chances of having a carrot and a fistful of sugar lumps in your pocket when you wanted to try and make friends with a couple of frightened horses attached to a hearse, eh? In Eddie's case, quite high, actually.

Sugar lumps were still considered an exciting innovation by Eddie's mother, Mrs Dickens (or 'that nice Mrs Dickens' to her friends), even though they'd been around since 1790. To her, they were one of the many marvels of the age, like gas lighting. No more candles! Simply turn the gas tap, light the gas and – hey presto! – instant light. (Knock the gas tap on with your top hat, don't light the gas and hsssssssssssssssssssssssssssssssssssssssssss, big explosion sooner or later.) Sugar lumps . . . sugar in a perfect cube. How's it done? Who knows? *Why*'s it done? Because we can! Eddie's mother loved gimmicks, and sugar lumps certainly fell into that category. She had recently insisted that Eddie carry a fistful with him everywhere.

The carrot was for a more practical purpose. Mr Dickens (Eddie's father) thought that a boy of Eddie's age should carry a knife with him for protection and for whittling. Mrs Dickens thought that Eddie might cut himself, so a compromise was reached. Eddie would carry a carrot for protection

10

and for whittling instead. Eddie knew better than to argue. Anyway, he didn't feel he needed protection (having once organised a mass escape from an orphanage, single-handedly) and had no idea what 'whittling' was anyhow.

The horses smelled the sugar lumps and the carrot and suddenly looked a whole lot happier. Eddie *scrunch-scrunch-scrunched* over to them with increasing confidence, and started to feed them the treats, patting their muzzles and muttering what he hoped were encouraging words.

Much to Eddie's amazement, Mad Uncle Jack had stuck to his side of the plan and was successfully pushing the coffin back into the glass-sided hearse without a hitch.

'There,' said Mad Uncle Jack. 'All done.'

At that precise moment, there was an enormous explosion, the sound of shattering glass and a plume of smoke appeared above the proud rooftops of Awful End.

Waking early to the sound of scrunching gravel, Eddie's father, Mr Dickens, had struck a match to light his first cigar of the day – he had recently taken to smoking boxes of the things to improve his cough – but had ignited some escaped gas. The hsssssssssssssssssssssssssssssssssssss had turned to BOOOOOOOOOOOOOOOOOOOOOOOM!!!

11

Episode 2

BOOOOM!

*In which someone or something
flips his lid*

Even the calmest of horses, with a mouthful of carrot or sugar lumps, isn't going to take kindly to a massive explosion. This black-plumed pair had been on the unnerved side of uneasy before the BOOOOM . . . now they were tearing off halfway down the drive, with the hearse in tow.

Mad Uncle Jack hadn't actually had time to twist the catch on the back of the carriage, and the coffin shot out of the hearse like a half-hearted cannonball from a cannon packed with not quite enough gunpowder.

It hit the gravel with a thud but, much to Eddie's relief, didn't split open to reveal its occupant. All of this seemed to have happened in an instant but, now that he had his wits about him, Eddie turned and ran inside the house to see if anyone had been hurt.

His mother was coming down the stairs with a stunned look on her face and the tattered remains of his father's nightcap in her hand.

'What happened, mother?' asked Eddie, running over to her and helping her to a chair. 'Are you all right? Where's father?'

Mrs Dickens pointed to her ears. Mad Uncle Jack would have taken that to mean that she was telling him that Mr Dickens was *in* her ears, but Eddie knew better. His mother was trying to tell him that she couldn't hear. The BOOOM must have affected her hearing.

'W-A-I-T H-E-R-E,' Eddie said very loudly and very slowly, then dashed up the stairs two at a time to see if he could find his father. When he reached his parents' bedroom, next to his own – or, more accurately, when he reached where his parents' bedroom should have been, next to where his own bedroom should have been – Eddie found . . . found . . . Well, it's rather difficult to describe, really.

He found a smouldering mess. Everything seemed to have been blown apart. Nothing was whole. There were bits of chairs, bits of wardrobes, bits of chamber pots, bits of bits and bits of bits of bits. And a slipper. His father's slipper, with a wisp of smoke coiling out of it, as if on cue. Where the outside wall had been was now just outside . . . a huge gaping hole opening onto the back garden and morning sky.

There was a thud. Not a heavy thud, like the one when the coffin had hit the gravel on the driveway. This was more of a mini-thud. The thud of an unsmoked cigar falling from the rafters.

Eddie looked up. There, where the ceiling had once been, were exposed roof beams and, straddled across one, like an outsized kid on a rocking horse, was Mr Dickens, in nothing but a nightshirt.

Eddie's heart leapt for joy. Suddenly nothing else mattered. His father was alive.

'It's a miracle!' shouted Eddie at the top of his voice. 'It's a miracle.'

Though even more deafened by the explosion than his good lady wife had been, Mr Dickens could hear his son's cries of joy. 'A miracle? Not really,' said Mr Dickens philosophically. 'It'd be a bit sad to kill one of us off in Episode Two . . . maybe in a tragic climax, but not in Episode Two.'

Not realising that he was *in* any Episode Two, Eddie had no idea what his father was on about, but he didn't care. Running into one of the rooms that hadn't been destroyed when the hssssssssssssssssssssssssssssssssssssssss became a BOOOOOOOOOOOM, Eddie returned with a pair of library steps. They were designed for wheeling in front of bookshelves, but his mother often took them into the bathroom to use for diving practice – she'd climb up them and jump off into the tub.

Eddie dashed up them and helped his father down off the beam. He was covered in a fine powdering of dust which made him and his nightgown look grey. 'Powdered ceiling plaster,' he explained. 'Someone must have left the gas on.' Apart from his (hopefully) temporary loss of hearing, Mr Dickens seemed little the worse for wear.

Mad Aunt Maud appeared in what would have been the doorway from the landing if the inner wall had still been standing. 'See!' she said, with a steely look of rage in her eyes. 'I told you no good would come of these rowdy parties.' Neither of the Dickenses knew what she was on about – Mr Dickens because he hadn't heard a word she'd said, and Eddie because Mad Aunt Maud never made much sense anyway. She marched off the way she'd come.

It was only later that Eddie realised that was one of the few occasions since he'd met his great-aunt when she hadn't been carrying Malcolm, her stuffed stoat.

Back in the hallway, Eddie's parents were reunited. Unable to see her husband up in the rafters and unable to hear his cries, Mrs Dickens had assumed that he'd been blown to bits . . . To find him alive was the best thing that could happen before breakfast. There was plenty of hugging and kissing. This is always embarrassing to watch if it's your own parents doing it, and even more so in those days for some reason, so Eddie hurried back outside, leaving them to it.

He found Mad Uncle Jack in the driveway issuing instructions to the servants – ex-footsoldiers once under his command in some faraway place in some long-forgotten war – whose job it would be to clear up the mess. Eddie suggested that they also be given strict instructions *not* to light any fires or make any sparks until the gas pipes damaged in the explosion were repaired.

Mad Uncle Jack looked at him admiringly. 'I can see why Colonel Marley was glad to have you at his side at the Fall of St Geobad, my boy,' he beamed proudly.

Eddie was about to say something, but decided against it.

Mad Aunt Maud appeared, pushing between them. 'I said such rowdiness would end in tears,' she muttered, stomping off around the east side of Awful End, back to Marjorie, her hollow cow.

'Where's Malcolm, Mad Uncle Jack?' Eddie asked.

'Malcolm?'

'Her stoat.'

'I believe her stoat's name is Sally,' said Mad

Uncle Jack, which was a common error on his part, unless, of course, it was Mad Aunt Maud who consistently got the name wrong. 'Is that her?' He pointed at a stone birdbath on a pedestal. In it was Malcolm, floating on his back. It was a strange morning all round.

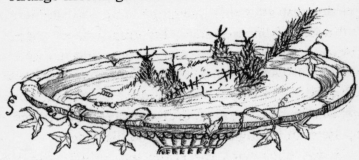

Relieved that no one was injured from the explosion, Mad Uncle Jack and Eddie returned their attention to the lonely coffin lying further down the driveway.

'What's your father's gentleman's gentleman called?' asked Uncle Jack.

'Dawkins,' said Eddie. Dawkins had moved to Awful End with Eddie and his parents, along with a failed chambermaid called Gibbering Jane.

'I thought it was something like Daphne,' said Mad Uncle Jack, a thin, puzzled frown fighting to find enough space to fit on his thinnest of thin faces.

'So does Father,' Eddie explained, 'which must be where you got the idea from.'

18

'Well, would you please go and find Dawkins and ask him to help us move this coffin to the stable block, where it will be free from casual discovery,' said Mad Uncle Jack. 'Who knows what distress it might cause your poor dear mother or my dear wife to stumble upon such a thing by accident . . . particularly after this morning's other events?'

Eddie was impressed by his great-uncle's clear thinking and complete lack of concern for the state of his property. He returned with Dawkins who, through years of training as a gentleman's gentleman didn't bat an eyelid at being instructed to assist in hiding a coffin in a stable block.

It was only when the coffin was nestling on a bed of straw that Eddie had time to read the inscription on a small brass plate screwed to the lid with four small brass screws. There were no dates for birth or death, just a name . . . but no ordinary name. It seemed more like a title, in fact. It read:

THE GREAT ZUCCHINI

Eddie felt sure that he'd heard the name somewhere before. Was it something to do with ice cream, perhaps?

In the days before people had learnt to harness the power of electricity, people didn't have electric fridges – I'll leave you to work out why – and ice cream was a new and exciting food brought over from Italy. It was sold in big towns and cities by Italians, out of little carts (a bit like prams) kept cool with big blocks of ice. The ice-cream sellers often painted their names on their carts. Eddie thought he'd probably seen the name 'Zucchini' on just such a cart . . . no, that wasn't it.

Eddie Dickens was so busy trying to remember where he'd seen or heard the name 'The Great Zucchini' before, that he didn't pay much attention to the creaking sound at first. Then he did. Especially when he realised where it was coming from . . .

The coffin was creaking. Correction, the *lid* of the coffin was creaking as someone was opening it *from the inside*.

To the Very Top!

*In which Mad Aunt Maud is hit
by a low-flying object*

The man who sat up in the coffin certainly didn't look very dead. Eddie was surprised to find that he was actually a little *disappointed* that the occupant didn't have a skinless skull for a head, or at least scary teeth. In fact, he reminded Eddie of Mr Collins who worked in the ironmonger's. He had a very round head with very little hair and sparkling eyes.

He looked very surprised when he saw Eddie.

'Where on earth am I?' he asked. 'Where are the crowds . . . Mr Skillet and Mr Merryweather?

21

Where is my Daniella?'

Eddie had no idea what he was talking about. 'You're in the stable block of Awful End, sir,' he explained politely.

'Awful what?' asked the man. He certainly didn't sound 'Great', or Italian.

'Awful End, sir,' said Eddie. 'The home of the Dickens family . . . I'm Eddie Dickens.' He put out his hand. The man in the coffin shook it.

'I'm the Great Zucchini,' said the Great Zucchini.

'You're not dead, are you?' asked Eddie then, realising how stupid he sounded, added hurriedly: 'I mean, you didn't think you were?'

'Whatever makes you think that?' asked the Great Zucchini, swinging his legs over the edge of the coffin and onto the straw.

'Oh, just little clues,' said Eddie, 'such as finding you in a coffin with your name on it, in the back of a hearse.'

The man nodded. 'A good point, young man. I see what you're alluding to. No, I went into this coffin very much alive and intended to come out that way, which is, as you can see, what has occurred. Unfortunately, instead of emerging to the applause and approbation of an eager crowd, I find myself in a private stable block with an audience of one.'

The word 'audience' made Eddie feel a little uneasy. He'd once had a run-in with a man by the name of Mr Pumblesnook – an actor-manager of a band of wandering theatricals – who had caused poor old Eddie nothing but Grief with a capital 'G' (which is how I just spelled it, anyway).

'You're not a wandering theatrical, are you, sir?' asked Eddie, trying to keep the revulsion out of his voice but failing spectacularly.

The man leapt to his feet and looked even less 'Great' and even more like Mr Collins, the iron-monger. Eddie noticed that what little hair the Great Zucchini did have – a patch just above each ear – was dyed black rather than naturally black. If the truth be told, from the smell of boot polish Eddie'd just detected, 'dyed' was probably too strong a word for it. Eddie suspected that the hair was *polished* black. The man was quivering.

'Indeed I am NOT a wandering theatrical,' he protested, and was obviously upset.

'I didn't mean to offend you,' Eddie assured him. 'I was simply trying to make sense of what you were doing in a coffin in the back of a hearse.'

'And I'm still trying to puzzle out how I came to be here,' said the Great Zucchini.

'My great-uncle woke me at six o'clock this morning to say that he'd found a hearse in our driveway,' said Eddie. 'He sleeps in a tree house at the rear but has excellent hearing and was probably aroused by the horses' hooves on the gravel. There was no driver and, by the time I came to look, your coffin was half in and half out of the vehicle.'

'Your great-uncle sleeps in a tree house?'

'Yes,' said Eddie, wishing he hadn't mentioned that part. He'd so have liked his family to be normal. He certainly had no intention of telling the Great Zucchini about Mad Aunt Maud living in Marjorie.

'And my hearse turned up riderless in your driveway?'

'Yes,' said Eddie. He led the man out of the stable block and over to the spot where he'd first seen the hearse.

'Where is the hearse now?' asked the Great Zucchini. Standing next to each other as they now were, Eddie realised that the man wasn't actually

24

that much taller than he was.

'There was an explosion in the house –'

'In the tree house?'

'In the main house –'

'An explosion?'

'Yes, and it frightened the horses and your coffin fell out of the back and we carried the coffin – you – into the stable, and here we are,' said Eddie.

'Here we are indeed, Mr Eddie Dickens, and what an extraordinary story it is too,' said the Great Zucchini. He slapped Eddie on the back.

'Would you be good enough to explain your part of it?' asked Eddie, as they scrunched their way up the drive towards the front door.

'I am an escapologist, young man. An escapologist. Do you know what that is?'

'Someone who studies pyramids and mummies . . . The kind in bandages, I mean?' Eddie suggested.

'You're thinking of an Egyptologist,' grinned the man and, when he grinned, he looked so like Mr Collins, the ironmonger, that Eddie half-expected him to try to sell him a box of screws or a new shovel for the coal scuttle because that's what iron-mongers do, you see: they monger iron. (And no, if the truth be told, I'm not 100 per cent sure what 'monger' actually means either.) 'An escapologist is a professional escaper,' he explained.

'I escaped from an orphanage once,' said Eddie proudly. 'Does that make me a professional escapologist?'

'Were you paid for it?' asked the Great Zucchini.

Eddie shook his head.

'Then I'm afraid not,' said the man from the coffin. 'Escaping is how I earn my daily bread. Anyone can escape – just think of all those convicts who keep escaping to the moors.' He looked in the direction of the nearby moors, neatly bringing them into the story and lodging them in the reader's mind for later. (M-O-O-R-S. E-S-C-A-P-E-D C-O-N-V-I-C-T-S. Okay? Good . . . as if you'd forgotten the brilliant picture of them on the cover.) 'The skill is to escape from something interesting in an exciting way, and in front of a paying audience.'

Mad Uncle Jack appeared at the side of the house and fished the stuffed stoat out of the birdbath. 'Your great-aunt wants Sally,' he said, on seeing Eddie. 'She's inside the cow. Take it to her, would you?' Then he noticed the Great Zucchini. 'Good morning, Mr Collins,' he said. 'I wasn't aware that ironmongers made house calls.'

The escapologist looked confused. 'You have mistaken me for someone else, sir,' he said.

'I think not, Mr Collins,' said Mad Uncle Jack.

'I would recognise your hair anywhere.'

'But I have no hair,' said the Great Zucchini. 'At least, very little.'

'Exactly, Mr Collins! Exactly!' said Mad Uncle Jack, as though he'd cleverly proved his point. With that, he thrust the dripping-wet Malcolm into Eddie's arms and marched indoors.

Eddie held the stoat by its rigid tail and let the water run off its nose onto the gravel: *drip drip drip*.

'I take it that that is your great-uncle?' said the Great Zucchini.

'Yes, sir,' said Eddie.

'The one who lives in a tree house?'

'Yes, sir,' said Eddie.

'And Sally?' asked the Great Zucchini, looking at Malcolm, with eyebrows raised.

'My great-aunt's companion,' Eddie tried to explain. 'A stuffed stoat.'

'It looks more like a ferret to me,' said the escapologist. 'Stoats have rounder noses.'

'Perhaps it was stuffed by someone who'd never seen a live stoat?' Eddie suggested

and, keen to steer the subject away from the strangeness of his relatives – I'm sure you know the feeling – he said: 'You were telling me about being an escapologist.'

'Indeed I was,' said the Great Zucchini, following Eddie, who'd given Malcolm one final shake and was striding off around the side of the house in search of Mad Aunt Maud. 'I specialise in Dreadful Acts – which is, in fact, the name of my travelling escapology show. I face death at every turn, escaping from a water tank filled with flesh-eating fish, from a flaming trunk suspended high in the air . . . but the great escape which brought me to this place was entitled "Back From the Dead" – a rather good title, though I say so myself. Mr Merryweather had suggested we call it "Arisen!" but I thought it too subtle.'

'Mr Merryweather?'

'My manager,' said the Great Zucchini, 'though I can't say that he's managed *this* particular escape very successfully!'

'What was supposed to happen?' asked Eddie. They wove through the narrow paths of the rose garden and emerged in a large area given over to lawn. Unfamiliar with Mad Aunt Maud's unusual living arrangements, the escapologist – with more than a passing resemblance to Mr Collins, the ironmonger – was surprised to see what appeared to be a giant cow in amongst some flowering shrubs.

'What was supposed to happen was that my assistant Daniella was supposed to bind me hand and foot, gag me and, with the aid of Mr Skillet, place me in the coffin,' he explained. 'The coffin would be screwed shut and placed in the back of a hearse. Mr Skillet would then ride the hearse, at a respectfully slow speed, with the audience walking behind – hopefully attracting more attention and more followers as others became interested and joined our most unusual of funeral cortèges.'

29

They had reached the back end of the cow, from which a crazy-eyed woman peered at them both through an opening. When she saw that Eddie was carrying Malcolm, she eagerly took her pet, stroking him between the glass eyes.

'Did Malcolm have a nice bath? Did he?' she asked. She suddenly noticed the Great Zucchini and glared at him. 'I know you, don't I?' she demanded in a voice that was enough to frighten an army of well-armed badgers.

'It seems that I bear a resemblance to someone named Mr Collins,' sighed the escapologist.

'The ironmonger?'

'Apparently,' he said.

'Ridiculous!' snapped Mad Aunt Maud. 'Mr Collins has great long droopy ears and shaggy fur. You, on the other hand, have no ears worthy of mention and certainly no hair, let alone fur. Ridiculous!'

'The one with great long droopy ears and shaggy fur is Mr Collins's cocker spaniel, Aunt Maud,' said Eddie hurriedly.

'Well, I know you from somewhere, I'm sure of it,' said Eddie's great-aunt, through narrowed eyes. 'What I can't remember, offhand, is whether I like you or not.'

'See you later, Aunt Maud!' said Eddie with false cheerfulness. He took the escapologist's elbow and steered him behind a box hedge. 'Forgive my great-aunt,' he said in a loud whisper. 'I'm sure she doesn't mean to offend.'

'I'm sure not,' said the Great Zucchini.

'Please carry on with what you were telling me,' said Eddie. 'It's most intriguing.'

'What was supposed to happen was that I would be taken to a field next to the churchyard of St Botolph's –'

'That's St Botolph's there,' said Eddie, excitedly. He pointed to a distant church spire, poking above a line of trees.

'We wanted the atmosphere of a churchyard for my great escape,' the Great Zucchini explained, 'but it would have been disrespectful to actually bury me in the consecrated ground of a churchyard.'

'You were going to be buried . . . in the ground?' gasped Eddie.

'That was the plan. Daniella and Mr Skillet were to lower the coffin into the ground, shovel earth on top and then erect a screen around it. A large clock would be started to indicate the exact amount of time it took me to escape, bound hand and foot, from my premature grave, to emerge from behind the screen. In the meantime, Daniella would keep the audience occupied, and the tension high, by playing stirring tunes upon a portable church organ.'

31

'Incredible!' said Eddie. 'Absolutely incredible.'

The Great Zucchini looked sad. 'This was to have been my crowning glory,' he said, the quiver returning to his voice. (What do you mean, you don't remember the quiver? I first mentioned it back on page 23.) 'Mr Merryweather had arranged for the gentlemen of the press to be present at the grave side. This was going to be bigger than "The Underwater Box" trick . . . more daring than escaping from "The Lions' Den" . . . and look what happened.'

'What did happen?'

'How should I know!' he quivered – see, it's spread from his voice to his whole body now – 'I was bound and gagged in a coffin with the lid screwed down in the back of the hearse. It's obvious that we never made it to the field by the churchyard!'

The Great Zucchini saw a garden bench and sat on it. He looked tired. Eddie had seen Mr Collins look like that after a hard day selling ironmongery, on one of his very rare visits to the shops. As you'll discover later, Eddie didn't get out much.

'Something must have frightened the horses,' Eddie suggested. 'They must have bolted and made off with you in the back . . . but how come you weren't bound and gagged back in the stable? And I thought you said the coffin lid was screwed down? You opened it easily enough.'

'For the very reason that I'm a professional escapologist!' said the Great Zucchini. 'I freed myself from my bonds within the coffin and unscrewed the screws from the inside. All I had to do was lift the lid off.'

Eddie sat down next to the escapologist and looked up at the gaping hole in the side of the house where he and his parents' bedrooms had once been. He was thinking. 'I can see how you might be able to open the coffin lid back in the stable block . . . but how would you have been able to open it with tons of earth on top of it? Surely that's impossible?'

The Great Zucchini gave Eddie a sideways glance. 'You're a clever boy, aren't you?' he said. And it didn't necessarily sound like a compliment.

'And what about air?' Eddie went on.

'Why does everyone go on about it!' cried the escapologist, leaping to his feet. 'So I have very little hair and, what little hair I do have, I dye! Is it a crime? Is it? I'm going bald and I dye my hair! Let's tell the world shall we?' He climbed onto the bench and shouted: 'I'M GOING BALD AND DYE MY HAIR!' Then he sat down with a bump. 'There? Happy now, Eddie Dickens?' he demanded.

'I said *air*,' said Eddie, in a little voice. He spelled it out: 'A-I-R . . . How could you breathe in a sealed-up coffin . . . You must have been in there for hours?'

The escapologist was obviously embarrassed about the little hair/air misunderstanding and pretended to find his shoes of sudden interest. He stared at his neatly polished toecaps instead of looking at Eddie when he spoke. 'Er . . . that's a trade secret,' he said.

There was a cough. He looked up. Mad Aunt Maud was standing before them. 'Ah, Mr Collins,' she beamed. 'How nice of you to come. I'll have half a dozen three-and-a-quarter-inch galvanised nails, please,' she said. 'There's a crack in Marjorie's udder and I want to repair it whilst the weather's fine.'

The Great Zucchini put his head in his hands and wailed. It was at that exact moment that the hot-air balloon skimmed the oak tree nearest to the house and came crashing to the ground.

Sent From the Skies

In which Eddie does rather a lot of dribbling

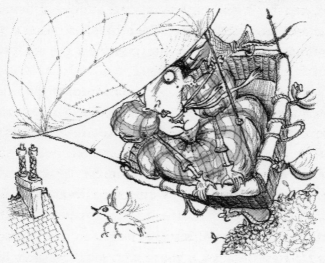

'How exciting!' said Mad Aunt Maud, dragging herself from beneath the basket of the crash-landed hot-air balloon and pulling the twigs from her hair. 'I can't say I ever imagined that I'd be hit by a hot-air balloon but, now that it's happened, I must confess to having enjoyed it.' She tore off the corner of a rhubarb leaf and pressed it against a cut above her eye. 'Really most enjoyable. Yes.' She crawled off into the bushes and back towards Marjorie, dragging a sprained ankle behind her.

Eddie and Zucchini took the accident far less calmly. You don't expect to be sitting in the back garden, quietly enjoying the sunshine and occasionally glancing through a hole in the wall created by a gas explosion, and suddenly have a balloon land with a crash right next to you.

Eddie's heart was pounding like a steam train and the escapologist looked as white as Mr Dickens had with all that plaster dust on him twenty-one pages ago . . . but it was the woman from the basket of the balloon who'd come off worse.

The balloon had come down at great speed, with the basket skimming the tree tops then dragging *through* the trees before coming to rest on the ground . . . though 'rest' is rather too nice a word for it. 'Rest' makes one think of relaxing under cool sheets in a shaded room on a sunny day with ones favourite cuddly toy. 'Rest' makes one think of 'having a little lie down'. No, the balloon didn't come to rest, the balloon came to a *sudden stop*, but its occupant didn't. The occupant of the basket became the occupant OUT of the basket (which, technically speaking, means that she wasn't really an occupant any more). She went flying through the air and landed in a rose bush.

Eddie had never seen anyone like her. He'd never seen a woman tangled up in a rose bush before, that's true, but that's not what I mean. Eddie had never seen a young woman with such a tight corset and quite so many layers of wonderfully frilly petticoats . . .

'Daniella!' cried the Great Zucchini, running forward to untangle her from the thorns.

'Harold!' cried the woman, in what novelists of the day would have called 'unbridled joy'. Because a bridle is something you put on a horse, it's hardly surprising that you don't find one on joy. And, anyway, this wasn't Joy but Daniella.

The name rang a bell with Eddie. What was one of the first things the Great Zucchini had said when he'd stepped from his coffin in the stable – after that bit about 'Where on earth am I?' . . .? 'Where is my Daniella?' – that was it.

Well, here she was, and what an extraordinary effect she was having on Eddie.

Okay, so crash-landing in a balloon and being catapulted into a rose bush is a pretty attention-grabbing way of making an entrance, but Eddie suspected that Daniella would have had a similar effect on him if she'd just strolled up to him and said, 'Good morning, Master Dickens.'

Most of the girls and women Eddie ever met wore dresses in such exciting colours as grey or black, or greyish-black. Not only that, these dresses began just below the chin and ended on the ground. Eddie was about nine years old before he even realised that his own mother actually had legs.

Yet here was this beautiful young creature – with a face a bit like the photographic plate of a camel Eddie had seen in a book called *Animals Other Than Horses Which Kick Too* – who had a neck, and ankles and lots of frilly bits under a tartan dress of red, blue and yellow . . .

'Are you an idiot?' asked Daniella, removing a snail from her ear and putting it back in the rose bush where it must have come from.

'S-S-Sorry?' asked Eddie.

'The way you're staring at me with your mouth open, and all that dribble?'

Eddie snapped his mouth shut like a clam and wiped the dribble from his chin with his sleeve.

There wasn't *that* much.

'This is Edmund Dickens,' said Harold Zucchini hurriedly. 'He rescued me.'

Daniella snorted. It was an enchanting snort, thought Eddie. It was the sort of snort that he imagined the beautiful camel in that book would have made. 'A kid rescued you? The world's greatest escapologist? I'd keep that quiet, if I was you.'

Daniella spoke with the sort of voice which shouted 'Bring out ya dead!' during the plague, or 'Who'll buy me luvverly roses?' in dreadful musicals about life in 'Good Olde London' in the time of Eddie Dickens.

This sounded strangely exotic to Eddie, who now spent most of his time at Awful End with his family, Dawkins, Gibbering Jane and an assortment of ex-soldiers. (More on them later, I expect.)

There was a lot of explaining to do, and Zucchini told his side of the story first. 'So tell me,' he said at last: 'how did I end up here in Awful End?'

Daniella looked at Eddie quizzically. 'Can I say in front of 'im?' she asked.

Zucchini sighed. 'I suppose so,' he said. 'The lad has as good as accused me of cheating anyway. He's guessed that, in the world of escapology, all is not what it seems.'

Daniella glared at Eddie. 'It ain't cheatin',' she

said, hotly leaping to Zucchini's defence. 'It's the tricks of the trade, that's what it is.'

'*Fuwuwuu,*' said Eddie, looking lovingly at the camel-nosed showgirl and trying not to dribble. Again.

'Are you sure 'e ain't no simpleton?' she asked.

'Just tell me what went wrong,' insisted the escapologist.

'Right you are, Harold,' said sweet Daniella, wiping her nose across the back of her sleeve.

★

Apparently, all had been going fine. The Great Zucchini had been ceremoniously loaded into the back of the glass-sided hearse and taken, in procession, up to the field next to St Botolph's. Of course, what the unsuspecting punters didn't know was that this was no *ordinary* hearse. No, this hearse had been especially constructed by Mr Skillet.

Once the Great Zucchini's coffin was on board and the hearse was moving, specially angled mirrors sprang into place that gave the impression that one was looking at the coffin but one was really looking at a picture of the coffin reflected back from the roof of the carriage. Meanwhile, the *real* coffin was shielded from the outside world. Under Zucchini's coffin was a secret compartment containing another, identical, coffin, and the two coffins could be swapped – one heightened and one lowered – by means of a rotating floor which Mr Skillet called the 'flip-flap'. So the coffin which ended up on *top* of the secret compartment and which was unloaded at the field contained nothing more than a couple of sandbags to give it weight.

I'm sure a diagram with lots of dotted arrows and 'Position A' and 'Position B' would be jolly useful here, but the Honoured Society of Escapologists forbids it, and I'm not about to risk waking up to find myself handcuffed in a trunk at the bottom of a river just so that everyone understands Mr Skillet's flip-flap.

(The sandbags adding weight to the other coffin had been sewn by the convicts at the nearby prison, by the way. They normally had to sew *mail*bags, and had sewn the *sand*bags specially, which was nice of them. Not that they'd had much choice. This had been before the mass break-out, leaving a number of escaped convicts up there on the moors – remember? – and the others locked up in their cells, with no more fun things, such as sewing, to pass the time.)

Well, you can guess what happened next. The coffin with the sandbags in it was buried and the screens erected around it, with the crowd thinking that the Great Zucchini himself was down there . . . and this, according to Daniella, was where things went wrong. What *should* have been happening in the meantime was that, with the hearse parked around the corner and away from prying eyes, Zucchini should have opened his coffin from the inside – just as he'd done in the stable block of Awful End – in the secret compartment, pressed a button flipping him and the open coffin back on top, and sneaked out of the hearse.

How he was then supposed to have got behind the screen so that he could appear to have come from the coffin and dug through the earth was deliciously simple, but Daniella had no need to reveal that part to Eddie. Why? Because everything had gone wrong before then. As Daniella told Zucchini (and the enthralled, drooling Eddie), the horses leading the hearse had bolted whilst the first coffin was still being buried.

'Suddenly, they rang the alarm bell at the prison because *more* of them convicts had escaped and it's really loud even miles away,' Daniella explained. 'It gave them poor beasts such a dreadful fright they ran, draggin' your 'earse behind 'em. John said he saw the back wheels go over such a bump that the mirrors flew back and your coffin shot up out of the hidin' place like a rabbit out of a hat.'

'Which is when I must have banged my head and knocked myself out,' gasped the escapologist. 'What happened next?'

'Well, there was the problem . . .' said Daniella.

The problem was that, interesting though a runaway hearse was, waiting to see if the Great Zucchini could escape from a coffin buried six feet underground was far more interesting, so Daniella and the others had to stay by the screens and pretend that he was down there whilst they decided what to do next. It was, as Daniella so neatly put it, 'a right pickle'.

'Me and Skillet 'ad a discussion in 'ushed tones while I played stirrin' music on me organ,' Daniella explained. 'John went off in search of the 'earse. He even borrowed an 'orse from the landlord of the local 'ostlery, but he couldn't find 'ide nor 'air of you.'

When she said ''ostlery' she meant 'hostelry' and, before you get sick to the back teeth of trying to decipher her words with all those letters missing at the front, I'm going to use a narrator's trick: I'm going to cheat. When I report what the lovely Daniella said, I'm going to use the whole words

43

and leave it up to you to imagine how she said them. I'll add a sprinkling of '''ere, what you lookin' at, mate?' now and then to remind you how she actually sounded, but it's up to you to remember most of the time. Fair enough?

'But the hot-air balloon,' said the Great Zucchini. 'Where on earth did you get the hot-air balloon?'

'I was just coming to that,' said Daniella, with a sniff. 'Merryweather –'

'My manager,' the escapologist reminded Eddie.

'Yeah, him,' said Daniella. 'If you remember, he invited Wolfe Tablet –'

'The famous photographer,' Zucchini explained to Eddie.

'Him,' nodded Daniella. 'Merryweather asked Wolfe Tablet if he wanted to come and take some photographs of your latest escape.'

'But I thought he wasn't interested? He failed to respond to the invitation,' said Zucchini. 'In fact, I seem to recall him saying that he thought I was a fraud and a charlatan.'

'Well, he does,' said Daniella, 'which is why he turned up in a balloon so that he could look *down* on the escape from above and see how it was done.'

The Great Zucchini's face reddened. 'The dirty rotten scoundrel!' he fumed. 'The lowdown good-for-nothing . . . I'd like to knock his block off! I'd like to . . .'

Eddie was worried that he was about to burst a blood vessel. The only time he'd ever seen Mr Collins look so angry was when one of the assistant ironmongers had muddled the three-quarter-inch nails with the half-inch nails . . . but he hadn't been half so furious as this.

Daniella mopped Zucchini's brow with the laciest of lacy handkerchiefs Eddie'd ever seen. He wished that it was *his* brow that she was mopping. (Sickening, isn't it?)

'Calm yourself, Harold,' she insisted. 'Nosy old Mr Tablet didn't get to see nothing because you wasn't there, remember. When his nasty hot-air balloon came sailing over the site where we'd buried you, he couldn't catch you sneaking behind the screen because you weren't around to do no sneaking. You was here, or in the hearse or wherever you was. But you certainly wasn't there.'

'Ha!' said Zucchini, with a triumphant snort. But Eddie didn't think it was nearly as pretty a snort as the sort of snort Daniella made. 'So for all he knew, I really was deep down in the earth inside that coffin!'

'Exactly!' grinned Daniella.

'Serves him right!' said Zucchini.

Eddie noticed black boot polish trickling out of what little hair Zucchini had left, and down his face. He'd worked himself into a right sweat. 'But

how did *you* get t-t-to be in the balloon, Daniella?'
Eddie asked, excitedly, doing his very best not to
dribble.

'Skillet and some of the crowd caught a hold of
his guy ropes that was trailing from the basket and
they pulled him to the ground. Most people
seemed to think it was part of the act and, when
they realised that he was none other than the
world famous photographer Mr Wolfe Tablet, they
was all interested in him and his equipment . . .
Havin' failed to expose any trickery and feelin'
right welcome, he agreed to go for a drink with
Merryweather and leave his precious balloon tied
up to a tree.'

'Overnight?'

'He had no choice. He kept on pestering
Merryweather to tell him some tricks of the trade,
so Merryweather agreed. Well, kind of. He bound
and gagged the photographer in his room at the
Rancid Rat and said, "Now get out of that!" He's
still there now, I suppose.'

'Pah! More fool him!' said Zucchini, with a
nervous laugh.

'Isn't he going to be a bit annoyed that you held
him prisoner, stole his balloon and wrecked it?'
asked Eddie.

Daniella was about to say something insulting
when Mad Aunt Maud came crashing back

through the undergrowth, in the distance, dragging her leg with the sprained ankle behind her. 'Peelers!' she cried. 'The place is overrun with peelers!' With that, she disappeared behind a compost heap.

'The police?' sighed Eddie. 'I wonder who they're after?'

Appealing to the Peelers

In which almost everyone
is in deep doo-doos

Now, I'm sure it's not true nowadays – though some of you are probably thinking 'He's just saying that' – but, in Eddie's day, most police officers seem to have been sent on a special course called Getting Hold of the Wrong End of the Stick. If it was possible to misunderstand something that someone – a suspect, in particular – was saying, then a peeler/police officer would take the *wrong* meaning.

Say, for example, you're a suspect and you say 'Good morning' to a peeler, the peeler will immediately ask: 'What's so good about this particular morning, ay? Done something to make yourself feel particularly good, now, have ya?' and you know full well that the 'something' he's thinking of is something illegal, like stealing a diamond the size of a plover's egg or kicking a chicken, and that he's hoping to nail you for doing it, simply because you were being nice and polite and saying 'Good morning'. For, as well as getting hold of the wrong end of the proverbial stick – which is like a real stick but, somehow, less sticky – peelers were particularly fond of nailing people.

Now 'nailing' in this context doesn't actually mean nailing as in 'nailing a bookcase together' (or even on your own), or even nailing as in 'nailing poor unfortunate people to crosses' (as the ancient Roman authorities liked to do), but 'nailing you for a crime' or 'pinning a crime on you'. In other words, being able to say 'You dunnit' (even if you haven't done it, but it'd be a bonus if you had).

Today people say: 'You can never find a police officer when you need one', unless, of course, they have found a police officer when they needed one, in which case, they'll probably say nothing. In Eddie's day, people would probably have said: 'What's that funny man in the funny hat and the funny uniform?' and pointed, laughed or thrown stones. Or all three.

Anyway or anyhow, with Eddie's limited experience from an earlier adventure, he had little doubt that, whether he told the complete and utter truth or a dirty sackful of lies, the peelers wouldn't believe him either way. At the station, he, Daniella and the Great Zucchini were taken to different rooms.

'Be brave, Daniella!' Eddie called out, as he was dragged in the opposite direction from the others. Because he was trying to sound brave himself, and because he was prone to dribble at the mere thought of her, his voice sounded very strange indeed. Daniella snorted and looked more indignant than afraid.

Eddie found himself in a small room with one table, two chairs and a mousetrap in the corner with a large piece of cheese on it, suitably old and smelly.

'This is the interview room,' said the peeler, 'so called because it's where the interviews take place, see?'

Eddie nodded, politely.

'Now I have some questions for you,' said the peeler, 'and I expect some answers.'

Eddie sighed.

*

Eddie awoke with a start, and with a starfish on his face. It was a full three seconds before he remembered where he was. When he did, he let out a groan, wishing that the peelers would do the same for him – let him out, that is.

There was a graunching sound and the door to the cell opened. In walked a peeler with a chipped enamel mug. From it hung a label which read:

PROPERTY OF HER MAJESTY'S GOVERNMENT

'What you need is a nice hot cup of tea,' said the policeman.

'Thank you,' said Eddie, accepting the drink.

'What you get is a lukewarm mug of water. What do you think this is, the Fitz?' The Fitz was a newly opened restaurant in London which was so posh that even the doorman was the Earl of Uffington and the washer-upper was a much decorated soldier – he had three layers of wallpaper under his uniform.

'How much longer are you going to keep me here?' asked Eddie.

'Have you heard of *habeas corpus*?' asked the peeler.

Eddie shook his head. (His own head, that is. He knew that shaking the policeman's head might annoy him.)

'Then we can keep you here as long as we like,' said the peeler.

'Would it have made a difference if I knew what *habeas corpus* was?' asked Eddie, suspiciously.

'Maybe,' said the peeler, hesitantly. 'Look, I must go. I just wanted to tell you that the inspector will be here to speak with you shortly.'

He left Eddie to finish his drink alone. The minute the door was shut behind him, Eddie felt flushed with guilt. He hadn't even asked about poor Daniella! What a worthless humbug he was. All he'd been thinking about was himself, when poor Daniella might be languishing in a nearby cell or worse. 'Wait!' he cried.

A tiny door opened in the top of the cell door, to reveal a glassless window. 'What?' demanded the peeler, peering through it.

'What about the others? Daniella and Mr Zucchini?'

'Wait until the inspector comes,' said the peeler, shutting the tiny door and stomping off down the corridor.

A moment later, a strangely beaky shadow was cast across the cell floor. Eddie turned to the small window, set high in the stone wall, and there was Mad Uncle Jack's face staring back down at him through the bars.

'All right, m'boy?' he asked.

'Fine, thank you, Uncle Jack,' said Eddie, 'except that I'm locked up when I've done nothing wrong.'

'Is that a starfish?' asked Eddie's great-uncle, pointing between the bars.

'Why, yes it is,' said Eddie. 'I found it in the bed, just now.'

'Pass it up, would you?' he asked. 'It must have fallen from my pocket last night.'

'Last night?' asked Eddie, confused.

'I came to speak to you at this very window, but you were sleeping. The starfish must have fallen from my pocket then.'

Eddie thought back to the electric eel that had fallen on him at the beginning of Episode One – not that he knew it was the beginning of Episode One, of course – and wondered, once again, why Mad Uncle Jack had taken to carrying *live* sea

53

creatures, rather than the more familiar dried variety.

He stood on the bed, on tiptoe, and passed the starfish through the bars. 'Many thanks,' said Mad Uncle Jack.

'What did you want to say to me last night?' Eddie asked, as he climbed back down onto the floor.

'Last night?'

'When you came to see me, but found me sleeping,' said Eddie.

'Did I?' Mad Uncle Jack frowned. 'I mean, I did?'

'You –' Eddie stopped. He heard voices in the corridor. 'The inspector's coming!' he said in a harsh whisper. 'You'd better go.'

'Very well,' said Mad Uncle Jack, 'but take this, quickly, just so you know that you're not alone.'

He slipped something out of his jacket and held it in his hand. Eddie jumped back onto the bed and took it from him, jumping to the floor just as a key clattered in the lock and the door to the cell swung inwards. Eddie looked to see what his great-uncle had given him.

It was the starfish.

The man who came into the cell with the peeler was as wide as he was tall and wore a very loud checked suit. Of course, checked suits can't really make a noise – except, of course, of material rubbing against material – but this was the kind of suit with checks so loud that if they could have talked they would have SHOUTED. It was the sort of suit that when, years later, television was invented, made the picture go fuzzy. Even when the man was standing stock-still, the checks on his suit seemed to be zinging all over the place saying – shouting – 'Look at me!' It wasn't a very new suit, Eddie noticed. The cuffs were a little frayed and the material a little grubby. He was relieved about that. The suit was giving him a headache just looking at it, and he was trying to imagine how much worse he'd feel if he'd had to look at a dazzling brand new one.

'This is the inspector,' said the peeler.

'I am the inspector,' said the inspector.

'The inspector would like to ask you some questions,' said the peeler.

'I would like to ask you some questions,' said the inspector.

The peeler gave the inspector a funny look out of the corner of his eye. To be fair, this was a deliberately funny look. Most of this particular peeler's looks were funny, whether intended or not, because he was a funny-looking peeler, but he really, really *meant* this one to be funny.

'Follow me,' said the peeler.

'Follow me,' said the inspector.

Eddie was led back to the room where he'd been interviewed or interrogated (or both) the previous day and sat in the same old chair. He looked over to the same old mouse hole in the skirting board and was pleased to see that the same old piece of cheese was in the trap, suggesting that the mouse hadn't fallen for it.

'Master Dickens,' said the inspector, who'd taken up position at the opposite side of the table but whose enormous stomach meant that the rest of him appeared to be sitting rather a long way away. 'Let me start by apologising for the way that you have been treated.'

Eddie was stunned. He was *Master* Dickens now, was he? And the policeman was actually apologising.

'You see, I would ask you to see things from our point of view. Firstly, a group of hardened convicts escapes from Grimpen Jail and are believed to be hiding somewhere on the moors. Secondly, the world-famous photographer Mr Wolfe Tablet is found bound and gagged in his room at the Rancid Rat. Thirdly, his hot-air balloon is stolen. You are aware of these facts?'

Eddie nodded. 'Yes, sir,' he said politely.

'Good,' said the inspector. His suit said nothing, but you could see that those loud checks were crying out to be heard. 'You also admit that you were found by the hot-air balloon in the company of one Daniella . . .?' He looked up at the peeler who'd been standing silently by his side since they'd sat at the table.

'No last name,' said the peeler.

'No last name,' repeated the inspector, 'who was not only seen in the stolen balloon by a number of eyewitnesses but has also admitted to being an accomplice of Mr Merryweather who attacked Mr Tablet?'

'Yes, the balloon crashed in my back garden. That is, the back garden of Awful End, my great-uncle's house,' Eddie agreed.

'Crashed, you say?' asked the inspector, sticking his little finger into his left ear and shaking it so violently that his whole tummy rippled.

Eddie noticed the peeler give the inspector another funny look – out of the *other* corner of his eye this time.

'Yes,' said Eddie. 'She – Daniella – landed in a rose bush. I told him all this yesterday,' said Eddie, nodding in the direction of the peeler. 'He wrote it down and everything. Didn't you read the report?'

'Mr Chevy's handwriting is poor and his

spelling atrocious,' said the inspector. 'What's more, I can't read.'

Eddie looked surprised.

'We haven't all had the advantage of a proper education, Master Dickens,' said the inspector, 'and, though no doubt useful, one doesn't have to be able to read to be an excellent detective inspector.' He gave his little finger another jolly good wiggle in his ear.

Eddie felt guilty again and cleared his throat. 'No, sir,' he said. 'Of course not.'

'Good,' said the inspector. 'Rather a coincidence, wouldn't you say?'

'I'm sorry?' asked Eddie Dickens, suddenly wondering whether he'd been trapped into something or other, but he couldn't quite see what.

'Rather a coincidence that Daniella should crash near the very spot where her employer, Mr Zucchini was seated.'

'Well . . . when I said crashed, I meant crash-landed. I mean she'd been on the lookout for the Great Zucchini and was trying to come in to land and –'

'Aha!' said the inspector, pushing his chair even further from the table, his weight causing it to grate across the floor. 'So she intended to land roughly where she did land and you were with Mr Zucchini?'

'Er, yes,' Eddie said.

'So you can see, Master Dickens, why we wrongly assumed you to be an accomplice in the taking prisoner of Mr Wolfe Tablet and the theft of his hot-air balloon?'

Wrongly? Had the inspector just said 'wrongly'?

'Y-Yes, I can see how you might have come to the wrong conclusion,' said Eddie, cautiously.

'Good,' said the inspector rising to his feet. 'So I do hope that you can find it in your heart of hearts to forgive us for holding you in the cell overnight.' He turned to the peeler, who Eddie – and you, dear readers – should already know was named Mr Chevy. 'The lollipop, please, Mr Chevy,' he said.

With a frown, the peeler dug his right hand into the pocket of his uniform and pulled out a round lollipop, covered in bits of blue fluff, exactly matching the colour of the fluff you sometimes find in your tummy button. (Don't think I don't know about these things.) He picked off the bits as best he could, and handed the lollipop to the inspector.

In turn, the inspector handed the lollipop to Eddie. 'Please accept this lollipop as a token of our regret for any inconvenience we might have caused you,' he said, patting Eddie on the head. Three times. Very awkwardly.

'Thank you,' said Eddie, quickly stuffing the lollipop in his own pocket. He had no intention of eating the thing.

The peeler disappeared from the room, returning a couple of minutes later with a piece of paper, a quill pen, an ink well and an old brown envelope containing the items he'd taken from Eddie before locking him up for the night: a few sugar lumps and the jagged stump of a well-chewed whittling carrot. (And if you can't remember what a whittling carrot is, I suggest you soak your brain in a mild vinegar solution overnight, or refer back to pages 10 and 11.) He handed them back to Eddie.

'We also need you to sign this special piece of paper,' said the peeler.

'We also need you to sign this special piece of paper,' said the inspector. 'What does it say?'

Eddie took it off the peeler. 'It says: "I, Eddie

Dickens, do not mind having been locked up overnight and will not go complaining to a judge, dot-dot-dot-dot-dot-dot",' he said. What it actually said was:

I Edy Dikuns doo nut mind haven bean locked up over nite and will nut gow cumplanin too a gudge
......

'What are the dot-dot-dots, Mr Chevy?' asked the inspector.

'They're the dotted line for Dickens to sign along, sir,' said the peeler.

'Good thinking!'

The peeler dipped the quill in the ink well and handed it to Eddie. He was about to sign when he stopped. 'I'll sign this, but only if you let me see Daniella first. I assume you're not letting her go?'

'Too right we're not,' said the peeler. 'She's a thief and an accomplice.'

'Then let me see her and I'll sign.'

'Promise?' asked the peeler.

'Promise,' said Eddie.

The peeler looked at the inspector. The inspector nodded. 'Very well, Master Dickens.'

*

When the door to her cell opened, the last thing Daniella expected to see was Eddie. 'Don't say they're bangin' us up in 'ere togever, two to a cell?' she groaned.

For a fleeting moment, Eddie was all excited at the thought of being locked up with her, then felt guilty knowing that he was about to walk free and she wasn't. How brave and defiant she looked, her nostrils flaring like those of a cornered horse, her . . .

'You didn't come in 'ere just to dribble and gawp, did ya?' she asked.

'No,' said Eddie hurriedly. 'They are letting me go, though.'

'And are keeping me 'n' Harold banged up, I suppose? That'd be right. An' they've already got poor Skillet and Mr Merryweather. That sounds fair.'

Eddie strode over to Daniella and gripped her hand. 'If there's anything I can do to help from the outside, just tell me and it's done,' he whispered.

Daniella wiped her hand on the back of her dress. 'You're all sweaty,' she said. 'And, yeah, you can help. Send me a cake baked out of dynamite.'

Eddie's face reddened. 'I'd love to do that . . . but I meant *legally* . . . Anything that I can do to help within the law . . . and wouldn't a cake made of dynamite explode if you . . ?' His sentence petered out and his face went even more red.

'Yeah, I was jokin',' said Daniella. 'Get that Wolfe Tablet to agree that he *asked* to be tied up, to see how Harold does his escaping tricks, and get him to say that he leant us the balloon. That'd be a big 'elp.'

'But how can I get him to do that?' asked Eddie, fearing failure.

'You're the bright kid who realised that the Great Zucchini couldn't really get out of 'is coffin with all that soil on top of 'im. You'll find a way.'

A loud checked stomach appeared around Daniella's cell door, soon followed by the rest of the roundest of round inspectors. 'Time to go and sign that paper, Master Dickens,' he said.

'I will find a way!' said Eddie. He took Daniella's hand and gave it a squeeze. His heart pounded. He felt like a hero in an adventure story (being totally unaware, of course, that he *was* a hero in an adventure story . . . though probably not *quite* the sort of adventure he was thinking of).

'You've got dribble on your chin,' said Daniella.

Making Things Better

*In which Eddie is faced with raspberry jam, an
ear trumpet and a very large moustache*

Back at Awful End, repairs were already under
way to the damage caused by the gas leak.
Unfortunately they were being undertaken by
Mad Uncle Jack and his team of incompetent ex-
soldiers who'd fought under him during a few
fruitless skirmishes on foreign soil, many, many
years before. They'd been incompetent soldiers
and now they were incompetent *ex*-soldiers, but
they were extremely loyal to Mad Uncle Jack.

Most of the men under Mad Uncle Jack had,
not surprisingly, been killed – particularly those
who'd followed his orders. It was only those too

incompetent to carry out the simplest of orders – 'Catch the next shell as it comes over before it harms anyone, there's a good chap,' or: 'Ask that man over by that cannon to stop firing, would you?' or 'CHARGE!!!' – who'd survived. There had been seven survivors, but two had since died, which left five ex-soldiers, Dawkins and Mad Uncle Jack himself doing the building work. Gibbering Jane was in charge of refreshments.

Mad Uncle Jack was delighted at his great-nephew's return. 'So they let you go, did they? . . . Or did you escape? Escaping from cells isn't becoming a habit now, is it?'

'They were *rooms* at St Horrid's,' reminded Eddie, referring to his earlier adventures in a previous book. 'And, this time, the peelers let me go. I was innocent!'

'Of course you were, my dear boy! Of course . . .' Mad Uncle Jack placed his trowel on the brickwork he was supposedly repairing. 'You haven't seen my missing starfish have you, Edmund?'

'Why yes,' said Eddie, 'and I've discovered that he's rather partial to lollipops.' Sure enough, as Eddie carefully removed the starfish from his pocket, one of its five arms was clutching the lolly stick and Eddie could have sworn he heard the faintest slurping noise.

'Excellent!' said Mad Uncle Jack. 'I must return him to the rock pool I've built in my study.' He hurried off.

'He's built a rock pool in his study?' said a bemused Eddie, though nothing should have surprised him in that house.

'Yes, Master Edmund,' said a rather dusty and very incompetent ex-corporal still in uniform (without the jacket). 'We helped him build it the other week. Dug up the floor and everything.'

Eddie had a sudden thought. 'You weren't at Colonel Marley's side at the Fall of St Geobad, were you?' he asked. 'Any of you?'

There were murmurings of 'What's St Geobad?' as though he was somehow accusing them of knocking it down.

'Never mind,' said Eddie. 'Er, what are you using as mortar to bond these bricks together?'

'Your Mad Uncle Jack's special mixture!' said the slightly dusty and very incompetent ex-corporal.

'It's jam, isn't it?' said Eddie, running his finger along the raspberry-coloured goo between the new bricks.

'It might have jam *in* it, Master Dickens,' said the ex-corporal.

Eddie tasted it. 'It's *just* jam, isn't it?'

'Jam might be a part of your Mad Uncle Jack's secret bonding formula.'

'It's just jam and nothing more, isn't it? No preservatives. No cement. No mortar. Just raspberry jam.'

The incompetent ex-corporal nodded. 'Yes,' he said, 'from a seven-pound earthenware jar he found in the pantry.'

'And it's not really going to repair this huge hole in the side of the house, is it?' said Eddie.

'Well . . . er . . . no,' agreed the ex-soldier. 'But we are just carrying out orders.'

Eddie sighed and decided to go in search of his parents. He found his father, Mr Dickens, in the library. This was a fantastic room with shelves taking up every inch of every wall (except where there were windows, otherwise it would have been – you guessed it – pitch-black). Even the doors had shelves on them, with carved and painted wood to look like rows of book spines.

Eddie's father was sitting in a high-backed leather chair and was reading a copy of *PUNCH*, a new periodical about bare-knuckle fighting. A periodical is just another name for a magazine. Bare-knuckle fighting is boxing without boxing gloves, which isn't much fun for the fighters – it hurts much more – or for the boxing-glove manufacturers, who don't get to sell so many pairs.

He looked up as his son entered. 'Hullo, Edmund,' he said. 'How was prison?'

'It was only a police cell, Father,' said Edmund, respectfully. There were no Social Services Departments back then, so children had to respect their parents in case they decided to lock them in a flooded cellar or tie them to the mast of a ship, without a social worker coming along saying 'Er, you can't do that!'

'Good, good,' nodded Mr Dickens. Although he'd had several baths since the explosion, he still had a pale and dusty look about him as though he'd been made up to look like a music-hall ghost. (Music hall was cheap theatre with plenty of songs.)

'How are you feeling, Father?' asked Eddie.

'Good. Good,' nodded his father.

'Oh, good,' said Eddie. 'I was looking for Mother. Do you know where she is?'

'Good. Good,' nodded his father. It was then that Eddie realised that he must still be very deaf after being blown up into the rafters just the previous morning.

'W-H-E-R-E'-S M-O-T-H-E-R?' Eddie repeated, very loudly and very slowly this time.

If this had been a public library, a stern librarian would have gone 'Sshh!' and pointed to a big sign which read 'SILENCE'. But this was simply a private library in Awful End so . . .

'Sshh!' said a stern man, pointing to a big sign which read 'SILENCE'.

So much for the all-knowing narrator. Sorry.

Because all the wall space was taken up by book spines – both real and wooden – the man had to hold up the wooden-framed SILENCE sign, which slightly lessened the effect.

'Who on earth are you?' asked Eddie, in loud amazement. He thought he knew all the strange people who worked on his great-uncle's estate.

'I'm your father!' said a puzzled Mr Dickens, whose back was to the man, so he'd neither seen nor heard him.

'Not you, Father,' said Eddie. 'Him.'

Unfortunately, Mr Dickens didn't hear his son's explanation, so was mightily confused, until the man came into view. He handed Mr Dickens what to you and me would have looked like one of those large brass horns that come out of the front of those old-fashioned wind-up gramophones you see in films . . . but which wouldn't have looked like that to Eddie or his father because wind-up gramophones and films were yet to be invented. The man stuck the small end of the horn into a startled Mr Dickens's ear.

'If I loan your father this ear trumpet then there is no need for anyone to shout,' said the man, speaking directly into the brass horn. 'I have been given

70

the responsibility of cataloguing this entire library and I cannot be expected to do so, in the time allotted, if I am to suffer constant interruptions. Silence or, at the very least, hushed voices would, therefore, be very much appreciated.'

'I can hear!' said Mr Dickens, clasping the ear trumpet. 'I can hear!' he repeated, much louder this time. He gave a whoop of delight and, like any whoop of delight, it was LOUD, which greatly distressed the man.

'Please!' he begged. 'A little quiet.'

Eddie looked at him. He wasn't much taller than Eddie and seemed to be mostly moustache. He wore pinstripe trousers and a black waistcoat and jacket, both of which were a bit shiny with wear. He had very little hair on the *top* of his head – though the moustache more than made up for that lower down – and what little hair he did have, he'd tried to brush across his bald patch.

'I'm Eddie Dickens,' said Eddie. 'This is my father, Mr Dickens. We're the great-nephew and nephew of Mad Uncle Jack, who owns this house . . . Did *he* ask you to catalogue all these books?' There was doubt in Eddie's voice because he couldn't imagine Mad Uncle Jack arranging for something so sensible . . . not the man who was, at that very moment, supervising the repairs to his house using raspberry jam!

71

'My name is Mr Lalligag and I was employed by the lady of the house,' said the man.

If Eddie had been puzzled and surprised before, he was stunned now. Even Madder Aunt Maud had employed a librarian to catalogue all the books in the library? That was about as likely as her having a sensible conversation with him. She lived in a hollow cow in the garden! Her best friend was a stuffed stoat which looked more like a stuffed ferret! Eddie was surprised she'd even remembered there was a library in the house!

'When did you start?' asked Eddie.

'This very morning,' snapped Mr Lalligag. Eddie thought the librarian would have made a very good ventriloquist because he couldn't see the man's lips move behind that most enormous of enormous moustaches. 'Now, I would be most grateful if you would keep the noise down!' With that, he turned and walked behind a stack of books, which was where he must have been when Eddie'd first come into the room and why he hadn't seen him.

'What a strange fellow,' said Mr Dickens. 'Rude, in fact. But this ear trumpet could be useful. Very useful indeed.' He returned his attention to his copy of *PUNCH*.

'Where's mother?' asked Eddie.

'About eleven thirty,' said his father.

There was once a famous author named Charles Dickens – no blood relation to our Eddie Dickens in these adventures – who used to fill his books with masses and masses of characters with very silly names. Because his books were so long, it often became quite difficult to remember who was who, so he got around this by printing a list of all his characters at the front of each book, under the heading 'CHARACTERS' or 'DRAMATIS PERSONAE' (which is Latin for 'DRAMATIS PERSONAE').

What with all these different people, such as Mr Lalligag, getting involved in *Dreadful Acts* so late in the day, I'm beginning to wish that we'd had one of those lists at the beginning of *this* book, but who's to say that we can't have one over halfway through this adventure? Who knows, it might even catch on. In fact, it makes more sense, because you'll already have read about the people I mention whereas, if this went at the front, you'd have forgotten who half the people were by the time you actually came across them on the page. Good thinking, huh?

Excellent. That's settled then. We'll have our list right here . . .

DRAMATIS PERSONAE

EDDIE DICKENS – *the hero*

MR & MRS DICKENS – *his parents*

DAWKINS – *Mr Dickens's gentleman's gentleman*

GIBBERING JANE – *an unqualified chambermaid*

MAD UNCLE JACK – *owner of Awful End, where all of the above live*

EVEN MADDER AUNT MAUD – *his wife, who lives with Malcolm inside Marjorie in the rose garden*

MALCOLM – *a stuffed stoat, sometimes called Sally*

or

SALLY – *a stuffed stoat, usually called Malcolm*

MARJORIE – *a large hollow cow*

MR CHEVY – *a peeler*

THE GREAT ZUCCHINI – *an escapologist*

DANIELLA – *his lovely assistant*

MR SKILLET – *his props builder*

MR MERRYWEATHER – *his manager*

MR WOLFE TABLET – *the famous photographer*

MR COLLINS – *the ironmonger*

THE DETECTIVE INSPECTOR – *a detective inspector*

MR LALLIGAG – *who says he's a librarian*

PLUS

an assortment of ex-soldiers, and the escaped convicts up on the moors

Not bad, huh? It looks quite classy, if the truth be told, as well as being a useful reminder of some of the characters we met so long ago you probably forgot about them. Speaking of forgetting, wasn't Eddie supposed to be doing all he could to convince Wolfe Tablet to drop the charges, not looking for his mummy?

The next place Eddie looked was in the kitchens of Awful End. Ever since she and Eddie's father had been cured of a very strange and smelly ailment, his mother was very particular about what she ate. When Eddie walked into the large, basement room, he found her talking to Dawkins, his father's gentleman's gentleman.

'Hello, Dawkins,' said Eddie.

'Master Edmund,' said Dawkins, with a slight bow. He was wearing a blue-and-white striped apron over his suit and was drying Malcolm the stuffed stoat with an Irish linen tea towel. Eddie deduced that Even Madder Aunt Maud must be close by.

'Mother –' Eddie began.

'One moment, dear,' said Mrs Dickens, whose hearing seemed to have recovered a lot quicker than his father's. She was seated at the huge kitchen table, sorting broad beans into two separate piles: small and not-quite-so-small. She graded them by passing each bean through her wedding ring, which she'd slipped off her finger specially. Those that passed through the thin band of gold went on the 'small' pile. Those that didn't fit through, or might have done but could have got[ten] a little squashed in the process, went on the 'not-quite-so-small' pile. When Eddie arrived, the 'small' pile was not quite so small as the 'not-quite-so-small' pile – in case you're taking notes.

'I'm discussing tonight's menu with Dawkins, my love,' she said. 'I will be with you in one moment.'

Eddie was only too aware that his mother's conversations were inclined to get rather long and convoluted, which is a polite way of saying 'very confused indeed'. He tried to explain the urgency of his mission with a 'But I need to get Daniella and Mr Zucchini –' but Mrs Dickens would have none of it.

'Sssh! Edmund,' she said, raising both hands for silence. In the process, she sent her wedding ring flying towards Dawkins (who was carefully drying Malcolm's eyes with the corner of the tea towel) and sent a broad bean flying towards Eddie.

It hit him smack in the eye. Sure, it would have been more painful if it'd been a bullet or even a small rock but, boy, did it hurt.

'Ouch!' Eddie cried out, though he was probably thinking some very rude words inside his head.

'NO!' screamed his mother, as her wedding ring bounced off Malcolm's leathery nose and headed for . . .

You're not going to believe what happened next. Even if you'd actually been there, you might have suspected that the whole thing had been rehearsed a dozen times to get it just right. If you saw it on stage, you'd clap at the skill and timing of it. If you saw it on film, you might turn to the person next to you and say: 'I wonder how many times they had to film this sequence to get it right?' If you watched it on video or DVD, you might pause it to see if there was any trick photography or careful editing . . .

. . . because Mrs Dickens's wedding ring bounced off Malcolm's nose and went straight into the gaping mouth of Even Madder Aunt Maud, who'd, at that precise moment, entered the kitchen yawning, following one of the many 'little lie-downs' she'd had since being hit by Wolfe Tablet's stolen hot-air balloon.

She was so startled that she let out a 'GULP!' of surprise and, with that gulp, she swallowed the ring.

'My wedding band!' cried Eddie's mother, not referring to Mrs Jonah Widdlington's – no sniggering, please; that was her name – String Quartet, who'd played at her wedding reception – but to her wedding *ring*, which was now on its long and unpleasant journey to Even Madder Aunt Maud's stomach and beyond.

'What are you trying to do?' Even Madder Aunt Maud demanded. 'Poison me?'

Seconds later, she found Eddie's mother's hands around her neck. Mrs Dickens was trying to make her cough up the ring, but Even Madder Aunt Maud didn't know that. As far as she was aware, someone had tossed some foul-tasting pill into her mouth the very second she'd entered the kitchen, and now someone was trying to strangle her.

What upset her the most, though, was that she was sure that the pill had come from the direction of Malcolm. Was Malcolm – her dear, beloved, Malcolm – in on the plot to kill her? Tears sprang to her eyes as Mrs Dickens continued to give her neck a good shake.

Dawkins placed the stuffed stoat on the table and did his best to separate the two women as politely as possible, being only too aware that these were the ladies of the house and he was merely a gentleman's gentleman.

'Cough it up, Maud!' Mrs Dickens was shouting.

'*Et tu*, Malcolm?' said Even Madder Aunt Maud – whatever that might mean – doing her best to out-stare the glassy-eyed traitor.

'Ladies! Ladies!' Dawkins pleaded.

Eddie left them to it. It was clear that he was going to have to try to persuade Wolfe Tablet to drop the charges against Daniella and the Great Zucchini *all by himself.*

To the Rescue

*In which Eddie's attempt to rescue the others
results in him needing to be rescued too*

Wolfe Tablet had travelled to the area by
hot-air balloon, and that balloon had now
been impounded by the police 'pending further
investigations' and was going nowhere.
'Impounded' actually means 'held in legal custody'
but, in this case, it meant that the peelers had it
tethered to the ground on a small patch of grass
around the back of the police station (where they
usually played football) and were taking it in turns
to go up and down in it. One or two lost their hats,

a few were airsick but, all in all, they agreed that it was great fun.

Mr Tablet himself, meanwhile, was back in his rooms at the Rancid Rat, recovering from his ordeal, and it was to the Rancid Rat that Eddie was now headed. I've said it before and I'll say it again: Eddie didn't get out much. When he wasn't drawn into adventures that weren't of his own making, he spent most of his time at home. And home was now Awful End. He wasn't particularly familiar with the surrounding villages, towns or countryside. He didn't have a bike. There wasn't a local bus service, and there were no shopping malls or burger joints to hang out at with your friends back then. A trip to the ironmonger's to buy a hook for the back of the loo door was an event, and a very rare one at that. So Eddie would have to ask how to get to the Rancid Rat.

The best person to have asked would have been Dawkins because, as long as he had enough tissue paper, he seemed happy with life and was good and practical at most things. But he was still busy trying to calm Eddie's mother and Even Madder Aunt Maud. There was no point in asking Mad Uncle Jack for directions. He'd once started to draw Eddie a layout of the gardens, but it'd turned into a picture of a frog carrying a parasol, which he then proceeded to colour in with green crayon, cut out and pin to the wall of his study, with great pride – his original task completely forgotten!

Gibbering Jane was an ideal person to talk to if you had a query about knitting. What she didn't know about knitting could probably be written on the head of a pin, and still leave plenty of room for the Lord's Prayer and a list of your ten least favourite meals . . . but directions? Eddie wasn't 100 per cent convinced she knew up from down, let alone left from right, or how to get to the Rancid Rat.

As for Mad Uncle Jack's band of ex-soldiers . . . Eddie did another one of his sighs, and decided to set off and ask for directions from the people he met on the way . . . which is all fine and dandy, so long as you actually *meet* somebody.

An hour or so later, Eddie had to admit to himself what he'd been denying for the previous half-hour: he was well and truly lost. He wouldn't be able to find his way back to Awful End, let alone the Rancid Rat. He had somehow found his way up onto the moors.

If this was a film, I'd have a dramatic chord of music about now. If this was a book, I'd make it a dramatic end to an episode. Hang on. This *is* a book but, then again, Eddie didn't know that, did he? All he could see was miles and miles of grass, boulders, gorse bushes and the occasional blasted tree. (I'm not swearing. I don't mean blasted as in 'These blasted shoes are giving me foot-ache,' but blasted as in 'blighted or withered'. In other words, even the trees up on the moors were fed up and leafless.) He'd lost sight of St Botolph's and Awful End somewhere below, not only because the moors were undulating – went up and down a lot – and were hiding them behind a hill, but also because of the mist.

In books such as these (not, as I've just said, that Eddie had the slightest notion that he was in a book such as this, or any other such book) mist and moors seem to go together. In fact, misty moors are a must. Get a moor without mist and you feel hard done by . . . so Eddie got the full works, and completely lost.

If only someone would find me, he thought. He hated being up there on his own. But when some-one *did* find him, Eddie wished that the someone had been someone different . . . because out of the swirling mist loomed the most frightening human being Eddie had ever seen.

He was huge, for a start, with a neck as thick as his head, so you couldn't tell it *was* a neck, and a face covered in horrifying scars. They reminded Eddie of the stitching on Malcolm, where his sawdust stuffing was showing through. This monster of a man had no hair on the top of his flat-topped head, but the hairiest ears Eddie'd ever seen, and chest-hair sprouting from the top of his crumpled suit . . . a suit which looked more like a pair of ill-fitting pyjamas, with arrows on them.

If the arrows weren't clue enough, the giant was carrying a huge, black metal ball – as big as a pumpkin – on a piece of chain, the other end of which was attached to his ankle with a manacle . . . Eddie was left in no doubt that this was one of the convicts who'd escaped from Grimpen Jail.

The convict bent down and looked poor Eddie straight in the eyes. 'You ain't going to scream, are ya?' he asked, his voice deep and gravelly. His teeth were small and yellow and his breath smelled sour.

'N-N-No, sir,' said Eddie, polite as always.

'Good,' said the convict, 'or I should have to snap your neck in two, like a dried twig.'

'He would, too!' said another escaped convict, appearing out of the mist to Eddie's right. He'd moved so silently that Eddie did that almost-jumping-out-of-his-own-skin thing that surprised people do. 'That's why he's called Bonecrusher,' said the second man.

This second convict was almost as thin as Eddie's Mad Uncle Jack and was almost as frightening as Bonecrusher, but in a different way. He had long grey wisps of hair coming from his head and pointed chin, and had hooded eyes, which somehow reminded Eddie of a bird of prey getting ready to pounce on its unsuspecting victim. Staring into those eyes, Eddie could imagine a sharp brain behind them, cogs turning, hard at work.

'What are you doing up here?' demanded Bonecrusher, grabbing Eddie's arm. 'You ain't spying for the peelers, are ya?'

'N-N-No, Mr Bonecrusher,' Eddie assured him. 'I'm lost. I'm trying to find my way to the Rancid Rat . . . My friends have been locked up by the police and I'm trying to get them freed.'

'How very interesting,' said the second convict, with a grin. 'Come with us.' He took Eddie's other arm and, between them, he and Bonecrusher led him away through the mist.

A matter of minutes later – though it seemed an endless journey to Eddie because he feared it might be his last – he found himself being led into a small cave in a rocky outcrop. It was there he met his third convict.

A tiny man – he was smaller than Eddie – he

had a shaven head, big bushy eyebrows and wide open eyes that made him look more than a little crazy. Add to this the fact that he was jumping up at Eddie, barking like an eager puppy held in place not by a leash but by his ball and chain, and Eddie was left in little doubt that the man *was* crazy.

'This is Barkin',' said Bonecrusher. Barking gave a happy yelp and snapped at Eddie's ankles.

'I'm Eddie Dickens,' said Eddie.

'Forgive me for bein' so rude,' said the tall, thin convict, with a sneer. 'I failed to introduce myself. My name is Swags . . .'

'Short for Swagman,' explained Bonecrusher, his sour breath close to Eddie's face again, 'on account of him being one of the few convicts sent to Australia to make it back here alive.'

This caused much laughter between the convicts – well, more 'happy yapping' in Barking's case –

as so often seems to happen between baddies in stories, when they have a new captive.

Eddie decided that he'd better show them that he wasn't too afraid, or impressed. 'I know a man who can escape from tanks full of flesh-eating fish, and from locked trunks set on fire and –'

'You know the Great Zucchini?' demanded Bonecrusher, picking up Eddie by the arm with one hand, as though he weighed no more than a chicken, and plonking him down on a rock in the middle of the muddy cave floor.

'Y-Yes,' said Eddie, uncertainly.

'How?' demanded Bonecrusher, pressing his nose right up against Eddie's. 'And no lies.'

The unspoken threat left Eddie feeling chilled to the bone. He told the convicts everything.

'So you don't know where the hearse is now?' asked Swags, once Eddie had finished. Eddie shook his head.

'But he could find it for us,' said Bonecrusher, with obvious excitement. He was breathing faster, his huge chest heaving in and out. Barking jumped up onto the boulder and growled.

'I'm sure I could,' said Eddie with genuine eagerness, because he'd rather have been anywhere else in the entire world – including frightening foreign places – than right there right then. Reading about this might be fun for us, but it wasn't much fun for him living it!

'But what guarantee do we have that you'll come back once you've found it?' asked Swags.

'Good point,' nodded Bonecrusher.

Barking just whimpered.

'Er . . . I could give you my word,' Eddie suggested, not convinced that they'd be too impressed with this suggestion.

'I can see that you're a gentleman and that,' said Bonecrusher, 'but gentlemen don't usually feel obliged to keep their word when dealin' with the likes of us.'

'Escaped convicts and suchlike,' Swags nodded in agreement. 'So we'll need more than that to make sure you return.'

'But why's the hearse so important in the first place?' Eddie asked. 'If you want to escape from the moors, surely any horse and carriage will do. A horse and cart, even?'

Eddie found himself being lifted up by the neck, something which'd only been done to him once before (by a not-so-charming woman called Mrs Cruel-Streak) and that hadn't been half so frightening as it was now, having it done by an escaped convict in a cave, up on the misty moors when no one knew where he was.

'Don't ask questions, boy,' said Bonecrusher. It was just Eddie's luck that he wasn't one of those monsters-on-the-outside, heart-of-gold-on-the-inside villains you sometimes come across. Mr Bonecrusher appeared to be nasty through and through.

'Hang on, Bones!' said Swags, suddenly. 'It ain't the hearse we need. The second coffin ain't in it no more. The boy said they buried it . . .'

'And Zucchini's people were then arrested . . . You mean, it's still in the ground?' gasped Bonecrusher. 'I'd have thought they'd have dug it up and 'idden it back in the 'earse by now.'

'But the hearse bolted and Zucchini's people were arrested . . . I'll bet it's still six feet under.' (Six feet was how deep in the ground genuine coffins were supposed to be buried, though some lazy gravediggers were quite happy to stop at four foot six.)

'Where did you say the coffin is buried?' demanded Bonecrusher.

'Mr Zucchini said it was buried right next to the churchyard at St Botolph's,' said Eddie, once Bonecrusher had let go of his neck and put him back down. 'I don't know exactly. I haven't been there myself.'

'Well, we need you to find it and dig it up,' said Bonecrusher.

'And not run away and fetch the peelers . . .' Swags let his voice trail off mid-sentence. 'Hostage,' he said, at last. 'Hostage. We hold the boy hostage.'

Bonecrusher scratched his bald head like people do in comic books when they're thinking (but very rarely do in real life). 'How can we hold Eddie hostage at the same time as sending him off to dig up the coffin? Surely we need *another* person – a friend of his – to hold hostage while he goes off and does the digging? Someone else whose bones I can break if Eddie tries to doublecross us.'

'No, listen, Bonecrusher. I have a plan. We send the boy's parents a note saying that we've got their boy and, unless *they* dig up Zucchini's coffin and bring us the sandbags, we'll do him some serious harm.' Swag's face broke into a gappy-toothed smile above his nasty pointed chin.

'That's good, that's very good,' agreed Bonecrusher, 'but there are one or two details we needs to work out, right?'

'Like what?'

'Like how we send this message and what we send with it, to show we really have the boy.'

Eddie was hardly listening. He was worrying about the part of the plan where his parents received the note and were supposed to do exactly as instructed!!! Exactly as instructed? No one at Awful End could carry out the most straightforward instructions. These were his *parents* they were talking about . . . and what if Mad Uncle Jack or Even Madder Aunt Maud got hold of the note first, or if it somehow ended up in Dawkins's tissue-paper collection before anyone had a chance to read it? He couldn't have the convicts sending a note that his life depended on to Awful End. It was as good as signing his death warrant!

'Er, I don't think this is such a good idea,' he protested. 'You see –'

But Bonecrusher, Swags and Barking were in no mood to listen. They were too busy pulling off his jacket, shirt and trousers . . . leaving him in no more than his long johns.

'We'll send your folks your clothes,' said Bonecrusher.

'That way they'll not only know that we really do have you, but they'll also bring us the sandbags double quick so you don't catch your *death* of cold,' grinned Swags. They laughed some more.

91

In the Grip of the Enemy

In which Eddie is . . . in the grip
of the enemy

'Let me get this straight,' said Eddie. 'You want to keep me hostage whilst' – people used words such as 'whilst' in those days – 'whilst my parents go and dig up the coffin with the sandbags in it?'

'That's right,' said Bonecrusher, with a toothy grin.

'Even though Awful End may still be teeming with peelers looking for evidence against the Great Zucchini and Daniella, after the theft of the hot-air balloon and the so-called kidnapping of Mr Wolfe Tablet?' Eddie added, breathlessly.

'Quiet, you,' said Bonecrusher, his expression becoming the even nastier side of nasty. 'You're not going to trick your way out of this.'

Swags stared straight at Eddie through his hooded eyes. 'The boy might have a point,' he said.

'And even if the peelers aren't there and the message reaches my parents, surely you're letting even more people know your plan . . .'

'Go on,' said Swags, not taking his eyes off Eddie for a minute as he began to circle him, his chain chinking behind him.

'I mean . . . I don't know why those two sandbags which you made for the Great Zucchini are so important to you, but I now know that they are. Surely the fewer people who know that the better?' Eddie had their attention now. He had to do everything to make sure they let him go, and not give the occupants of Awful End a chance to muck it up, or who knew what might happen?

'Then what do you suggest?' said Swags, coming to a halt. He put a bony hand on each of Eddie's shoulders and, pressing his nose against the boy's, stared deep into his eyes. 'And no tricks,' he added, his voice barely louder than a deep breath.

Eddie shuddered. 'No tricks,' he agreed, and he meant it. He wasn't in the convict-capturing business. He'd get them their sandbags and hope beyond hope that they'd let him go. 'If one of you was going to take my clothes to Awful End, along with a note, and risk capture anyway, why doesn't one of you come along with me while I dig up the sandbags to make sure I don't escape, instead?'

Swags and Bonecrusher switched into thinking mode, trying to see the fault in Eddie's plan. Barking seemed more interested in sniffing a patch of thistles by the cave opening.

'Hang on! Hang on!' said Bonecrusher. 'The 'ole idea of someone else digging the 'ole instead of us is that there's somethin' slightly suspicious-lookin' about a man with arrows on 'is suit doin' anything, ain't there? If we wasn't worried about that, we'd go 'n' do the diggin' ourselves!'

'But here's the clever part,' said Eddie, hoping there weren't any other loopholes in his hastily devised neck-saving idea. 'Instead of sending my clothes to Awful End, why not dress Mr Barking up in them? They'll fit him. That way, he can show me the way to the village – I'm lost, remember – and then we can go to the field by St Botolph's churchyard and dig up the coffin together . . .'

'And what if anyone stops 'n' asks what ya doin'?' said Bonecrusher.

'The boy simply says that he's part of the Great Zucchini's Dreadful Acts troupe, clearing up after a trick that was cancelled following the arrival of Mr Wolfe Tablet in his balloon,' said Swags, who appeared to be having his ear licked by Barking, who was beginning to behave even more like an excited puppy.

The three convicts looked at each other. Bonecrusher nodded. Swags nodded and Barking gave an excited yap.

'Passed unanimous,' said Bonecrusher. 'We go with your plan, boy . . . but not until morning.'

Eddie felt so relieved that he wouldn't now have to rely on his parents or, God forbid, Mad Uncle Jack and Even Madder Aunt Maud, but he was still in a very sticky situation. And he wanted to get it over with.

'Couldn't we go tonight?' he suggested. 'Aren't most crimes more easily carried out under the cover of darkness?' He'd read that somewhere.

'Too dangerous, sonny,' said Swags. 'When the mist's this bad, it's impossible to find your way round 'ere at night. You could both end up in the bog.' He wasn't using 'bog' as a slang word for the toilet/loo/lavatory/bathroom, so there were no schoolboy giggles. He meant bog as in boggy marshland . . . earth that could suck you up so fast you couldn't get out, and so deep your remains might never be found.

That was good enough reason to stay put until daybreak, but Swags had another one all the same. 'The search parties are out in force at night,' he explained, "'cos that's when some of the other escapees are stupid enough to be on the move. If they catch so much as a glint of a lantern, they'll let the dogs loose.'

'Daybreak it is then,' grinned the huge mountain of a man that was Bonecrusher. 'That gives us a chance to get better acquainted.'

To make sure that Eddie didn't try to escape in the night, each convict wrapped the ball-end of his chain around him, so he went to sleep – or tried to – in the middle of a big metal knot. Barking lay curled up against his feet, like a young puppy, whilst Bonecrusher and Swags slept with their backs to him (one on the left and one on the right), all on the sandy cave floor. Swags was no fool. He used Eddie's bundle of clothes as a pillow.

It's doubtful that Eddie would have slept even if the chains hadn't been so heavy, the cave floor hadn't been so hard, Bonecrusher and Swags hadn't been such loud snorers . . . and Barking hadn't whimpered on and off throughout the night, and twitched his legs like a dog dreaming that he was chasing rabbits. No, the main reason for his wakefulness was fear.

Dawn couldn't come quick enough for Eddie, but the escaped convicts insisted he had breakfast before he and Barking set off to retrieve the sandbags. It consisted of a few mouthfuls of leaves and grass.

'You need to keep your energy up for the day ahead,' said Swags. 'That's what we've been livin' off. P'r'aps you could bring us back some food too, yeah?'

'I'll do what I can,' said Eddie, spitting out the mushy green ball of chewed leaves, when he thought no one was looking.

Now all that remained was for Barking to dress up in Eddie's clothes and they'd be ready to go. Bonecrusher had already removed the uprooted gorse bush he'd wedged in the entrance to the cave, to keep it hidden from the casual observer on the misty moors in the dead of night.

Actually, it was more a matter of them dressing Barking. He struggled a little and was terribly ticklish, which made it a bit like trying to change a nappy on an uncooperative baby (if you've ever tried that). Then there was the small problem of the ball and chain. They couldn't pull the trouser leg over the ball, so they pulled it up the chain and over his leg, leaving plenty of room for the remainder of the chain, and the big, big ball to hang out of the top, for Barking to hold, if he didn't want it dragging along the ground behind him.

(To tell you the truth, I wasn't sure how they did this, so – because that's the caring kind of narrator I am – I tied a piece of chain-link fencing to my ankle and tried to pull a second pair of trousers over the pair I was already wearing, without feeding the other end of the chain through, where the big metal ball would have been. Just then, the front doorbell rang and, because I was expecting an exciting parcel, I was in a hurry to answer it. Suffice it to say, I ended up in a terrible tangle, but can now see how they did manage to get Eddie's clothes onto Barking, ball and chain and all.)

It was time to go. 'Now listen up, lad,' said Swags. 'Barking here has an excellent sense of direction – a nose for it, ya might say – and he can outrun ya, ball and chain or no ball and chain . . . and he has a nasty bite too. So be sure to stick to the plan . . . and no funny business.'

'No funny business,' Eddie assured him, and they were off.

Swags was right. Little Barking could move at high speed. As he clutched the ball on the end of his chain, it did little to slow him down. Occasionally, he'd look back to check that Eddie was following and, if the boy did appear to be lingering, he'd yap at him. It wasn't that long before they were off the edge of the moors down into hedge-lined country lanes and, about an hour after that, Eddie suddenly realised where they were.

'I know the way to St Botolph's from here,' he said excitedly. Now it was his turn to lead the way, with Barking (wearing Eddie's clothes, remember) hot on his heels.

They cut their way through the churchyard, the morning dew dampening the bottom of Eddie's long johns, as they dodged their way between the tombstones littering the ground like broken teeth. Then they reached a low stone wall.

'There!' said Eddie, pointing to a mound of freshly dug earth over in the next field. He clambered over the wall and hurried to the spot. 'This must be it. It's about the size of a grave, and the amount of soil in the mound is about the amount of space the coffin must be taking up below.'

'*Dig!*' barked Barking, which was the first real word Eddie had heard him speak. If the truth be told, Eddie hadn't been convinced that Barking *could* speak.

But that wasn't what was making Eddie nervous all of a sudden. It was the fact that he'd just realised that there was a flaw in his plan. He didn't have a shovel or a spade or so much as a teaspoon to dig with.

'What with?' asked Eddie.

Without waiting to give an answer, Barking threw himself to his knees and began to dig with his front paws – sorry, that should, of course, be with his *hands* – like a dog desperate to dig up a treasured bone, small scoops of earth flying out behind him. Eddie started digging in a similar fashion down at the other end. This would take for ever.

This is hopeless, thought Eddie. He'd been digging for what seemed like ages and it was now the full light of morning, yet they hardly seemed to have made a dent in the ground.

'What in heaven's name are you doing here?' asked a familiar voice. Eddie looked up. At the moment he saw the Great Zucchini and the lovely Daniella in front of him, each with a shovel in their hands, he also felt something sharp in his back. Barking must have had a knife! One wrong word from Eddie, and Barking might do something very nasty indeed.

Escapes All Around

In which people seem to escape, or to have escaped, here there and everywhere

'Hello,' said Eddie, trying not to sound scared for his life.

'Whatcha doin' 'ere?' asked Daniella.

'I was about to ask you the same question,' said Eddie, looking up at the camel-faced beauty from his crouching position. 'The last time I saw you both, you were locked up at the police station.'

''E's the world's greatest escapologist, ain't he?' said Daniella, proudly. 'No local prison cell can 'old 'im!'

The Great Zucchini accepted the praise with a

slight bow, then his eyes fell on Barking, grinning at Eddie's side. 'Are you going to introduce me to your colleague?' he asked.

Eddie felt the tip of the object being pushed further into his back, out of sight of the newcomers.

'Er, this is Mr Barking,' he said. 'He's a friend of my Uncle Jack.'

'Why ain't you got no clothes on?' asked Daniella.

'Er . . . fresh air and exercise,' said Eddie quickly. 'My great-uncle is very keen on me taking more healthy exercise. Mr Barking is my trainer. I'm doing an early-morning run –'

'*Exercise ball*,' said a voice. It was Barking's. He handed Eddie the ball on the end of his chain.

Eddie dropped it with a thud on the earth, hurriedly picking it up with an idiot grin. 'Running . . . lifting exercise balls . . . er . . . digging,' said Eddie, helplessly.

'But why dig here?' asked the Great Zucchini.

'And how comes 'e's wearin' your clothes?' asked Daniella.

'Shut up,' said Eddie, desperately. He was running out of excuses!

'What?'

'Nothing . . . I mean . . .'

The Great Zucchini stepped forward and sank his shovel into the soil. 'Much as I would like to stay and talk,' he said, 'I need to get my coffin dug up and in the back of the hearse before the peelers find us gone.'

'*We'll help you*,' said Barking. The sharp pain in Eddie's back suddenly stopped. Eddie's eyes met the convict's. The words 'no funny business' went through his mind.

Eddie took the shovel off Daniella and started digging with the Great Zucchini, with Barking carrying on with his front paws – *hands* – as before.

If Eddie had been very brave, perhaps he would have hit Barking over the head with the shovel, but that's easier said than done. It takes a lot to bash somebody that way. What if you hit them too hard and split their head open by mistake? What if you don't hit them hard enough and they grab the shovel and hit you? So Eddie concentrated on digging.

Daniella sat on the wall. Even the sight of her frilly petticoats wasn't enough to stop Eddie worrying about what Barking might do next.

By the time they reached the top of the coffin, all three were a lot hotter and a lot sweatier. Eddie's long johns were streaked with soil, the boot polish colouring Zucchini's hair trickled down his cheeks, and Barking's little head was glowing red with all the effort.

Zucchini lowered himself down onto the lid of the coffin and Daniella threw him a coil of rope.

Quickly and efficiently, he tied it to the coffin, then Eddie and Daniella gave him a hand out. They pulled the coffin to the surface and laid it on the grass. Zucchini untied the rope.

'Skillet and Merryweather should be here with the hearse and the rest of my belongings shortly,' he said. 'The peelers found the hearse on the village green. The horses were drinking from the pond . . . They were good enough to put it in the stable at the back of the police station. Most convenient!'

'Then what are you going to do?' asked Eddie. 'You can't perform your Dreadful Acts if you're a wanted man!'

'I will either find a way of getting Mr Wolfe Tablet to drop the charges –'

'Something which *you* promised to do,' Daniella reminded Eddie, who blushed. If only he could tell her about the convicts . . . about who the harmless-looking Mr Barking really was.

'Or I'll send a large hamper to your local police station this Christmas,' Zucchini continued. 'It's amazing what peelers are willing to forgive and forget in exchange for a few bottles of port, a goose and some plum pudding.'

'*Open it!*' yapped a voice in Eddie's ear. Barking rattled the lid of the coffin.

'Could we open the coffin, please?' Eddie asked the escapologist.

'What on earth for?' he asked.

'What are you two up to?' asked Daniella. 'See, I knew you wasn't just diggin' here by accident.'

'Please,' said Eddie, looking directly at Zucchini.

'Very well,' said Zucchini, 'but there are only a couple of sandbags inside. It won't give away how the rest of the trick was done.' He crouched down beside the coffin and, producing something that looked like a cross between a corkscrew and a screwdriver, he undid the screws around the edges and, finally, lifted off the lid.

They all four peered inside. Sure enough, there were two large hessian sandbags labelled:

GRIMPEN JAIL

Just then, a commanding voice cracked the silence like a whip: 'Hands up, then nobody move!'

Eddie gave a silent groan. First Barking and now – now what? He looked up and was amazed to see Mr Lalligag, the man from the library! There was something very different about him since their meeting back at Awful End the previous day. He was still wearing the pinstripe suit and black waistcoat, slightly shiny with wear. He was still as bald as he had been, with what little hair he had brushed over his pate. He still had one of the biggest moustaches Eddie had ever had the honour of being that close to . . . but today? Today Mr Lalligag was holding an enormous revolver.

'Not *again*!' Eddie muttered and, if you've read the book *Awful End*, you'll know why. He, the Great Zucchini and Daniella all let go of the coffin lid and put their hands in the air. The lid thudded shut on the coffin, then there was silence.

'This place is gettin' busier than Piccadilly Circus,' muttered Daniella.

'Who have we here?' said Mr Lalligag, at last. 'Mr Collins the ironmonger, Master Edmund Dickens from the big house, and who might you be, m'dear?'

'Me name's Daniella,' said Daniella, ''n' what I wanna know is, what's such a small guy like you doin' wiv such a big gun?'

Eddie was so proud of her! She didn't seem in the least bit frightened of Lalligag. She turned to him. ''n' you can stop dribblin' and all!' she said.

'And I am *not* Mr Collins the –' Zucchini began.

'And, as you may have guessed, Master Dickens, I'm not really a librarian,' Mr Lalligag interrupted.

Now, before one of you readers gets all nasty and says, 'But you said he was a librarian in the DRAMATIS PERSONAE and if you, the narrator, can't tell the truth, then who can we trust?' I urge you all to look back at page 74, but keep your finger in this page so you don't lose your place. See? What I wrote was:

MR LALLIGAG – *who says he's a librarian*

Now, I can't be much fairer than that, can I?

'And you weren't really hired by my great-aunt to catalogue the books, were you?' asked Eddie.

'No,' Mr Lalligag agreed. 'The great thing about a house like Awful End is that nobody seems to know who's who or what anybody else is up to. Did you know, for example, that there's a woman living under the main stairs? She wears the top left-hand corner of a knitted egg cosy on a piece of string around her neck?'

'Of course I know. That's Gibbering Jane. She came with us to live there.'

'Oh . . .' said Mr Lalligag, obviously a little put out. 'Anyway, as soon as I learnt that the Great Zucchini was in the vicinity, I used a false identity to get into the house and keep an eye on what was going on.'

'So who are ya, then? If you ain't a librarian?' asked Daniella, decidedly unimpressed.

'I'm someone looking out for other people's interests,' said Mr Lalligag. 'Now, if you'll be kind enough to step away from the coffin, I'll take what I came for. Forgive this –' he waved the gun in the

108

air '– but I'm not sure who to trust, so keep your hands up, go over to the wall and lie face down in the grass. If any of you so much as looks up, I'll plug you.'

Though not familiar with all the euphemisms for shooting or being shot – a euphemism is a nice word or phrase replacing a nasty one so, for example, a euphemism for a three-hour exam might be 'a nice little test' – Eddie was quick to realise that 'being plugged' meant ending up with a bullet inside him; which is why he did exactly what Mr Lalligag had told him to do, and lay face down. Zucchini and Daniella did the same, which is why none of them saw what happened next.

They heard the cry, the barking and the clanking of chains, but it was only when they heard the excited yapping that they all looked up and worked out what had happened.

Standing in the open coffin was Barking, with a huge grin on his excited little face. Now *he* was holding the revolver, which somehow seemed even bigger in his tiny paw. Its previous owner lay slumped half in and half out of the coffin, and it was obvious that Barking had hit him with his ball and chain.

Mr Lalligag had opened what he'd expected to be a coffin containing nothing more than two harmless hessian sacks, to be confronted by a far-from-harmless convict, ready to pounce.

Now, the brighter readers amongst you – that's
37.2 per cent of you – will have been wondering
what happened to Barking all of this time and will
have been wondering whether I made a mistake. A
few of you might have been muttering things
along the lines of 'he must have got confused and
has suddenly written Barking out of the story alto-
gether. One minute he has the ex-convict there.
The next minute it's just Eddie, Zucchini and
Daniella.'

Of that 37.2 per cent, 26 per cent of you
believed that I hadn't, in fact, lost my marbles and
that Barking had managed to slide down the hole,
unnoticed, as Mr Lalligag approached. Only 14
per cent of the original 37.2 per cent of you who

noticed that Barking wasn't around guessed that he'd hidden himself in the coffin before the others had time to drop the lid and put up their hands.

I'm told by someone who doesn't get out much, and whose room smells of – well, I'd rather not talk about that – that 14 per cent of the 37.2 per cent of readers who noticed Barking had gone is just 5.2 per cent of all you readers . . . so, if you were one of those who realised where Barking had been all this time, please accept this well-earned round of applause:

Clap! Clap! Clap! Clap! Cheer! Cheer! Clap! Clap! Clap! Clap! Cheer! Cheer! Cheer! Clap! Clap! Clap! Clap! Cheer! Cheer! Clap! Clap! Clap! Clap! Cheer! Cheer! Cheer! Clap! Clap! Clap! Clap! Cheer! Cheer!

Right. That's enough. We don't want it going to your heads. Let's get back to the action:

'Well done, Mr Barking,' said the Great Zucchini, scrambling to his feet and striding over towards the coffin, unaware that he was now facing an armed escaped convict. 'Well done!'

Eddie leapt to his feet and took Daniella's hand, pulling her up. Touching her skin made him feel all funny in the pit of his stomach.

'*Who Skillet and Merryweather?*' asked Barking. He must have remembered Zucchini talking of their imminent arrival before Mr Lalligag had burst onto the scene.

111

'My manager and my props man. They should be here shortly,' said Zucchini. 'You can put that gun down now, my good man. The bonk on the head you gave this Lalligag chap has knocked him out well and good.'

'*Into hole please*,' said Barking, pressing the revolver into Zucchini's stomach.

'I don't understand . . .' the escapologist protested.

'He wants us to get into the hole,' sighed Eddie.

'*No. You with me*,' Barking told Eddie.

'Barking is one of the escaped convicts everyone's been talking about,' Eddie explained. 'We'd better do exactly as he says.'

The Great Zucchini and Daniella climbed into the hole while Eddie dragged the unconscious body of Mr Lalligag over to them and passed him in.

He then squeezed into the coffin with Barking, his ball and chain, the revolver and the sandbags. The situation was clear: one peep out of those three in the hole and Eddie would end up filled full of lead, or any other euphemisms you can think of.

★

Imagine the scene when Mr Merryweather and Skillet rode up the track beside the field, in the hearse Eddie'd first seen in the driveway of Awful

End, what seemed like ages ago. They were expecting to be greeted by the Great Zucchini and Daniella, carrying the coffin, all ready to throw it in the back for a quick getaway. Instead, all they saw was the hole, a pile of earth, the deserted coffin, and not a soul in sight!

Being on the run from the peelers, neither Mr Merryweather nor Skillet wanted to attract attention by calling out their missing colleagues' names, so they decided to collect the coffin and put it in the hearse, *then* go looking for them.

Of course, when they reached the coffin, Barking (who'd been watching their approach across the grass through a gap between the lid and the side) jumped to his feet and trained his revolver on the new arrivals.

'Blimey!' said Skillet, who had spent one or two years behind bars himself, for stealing a coat button. 'It's Arthur Brunt, the billionaire burglar!'

'Actually, his name is Barking,' said Eddie, getting to his feet. He had a stiff neck.

'He *comes* from Barking,' said Skillet. 'It's a place.'

Eddie looked at his captor with new respect. Was this man really the billionaire burglar the papers had written about when he'd finally been arrested and tried a few years back? He was supposed to be some kind of criminal genius. A mastermind.

Barking glared at Skillet, but then his expression changed and all pretence was dropped. 'How clever of you to recognise me,' he said at last. Gone was the strange yappy voice he'd used until now, to be replaced by a voice as smooth as silk: a *gentleman's* voice. He also looked different now. You know when a teacher says, 'Wipe that silly grin off your face.' Well, it was as if Barking had done just that. When he stopped grinning, his eyebrows lowered and he no longer looked like the puppy in the window of the pet shop which you just had to rush in and buy . . . He almost looked sophisticated; debonair.

'I do so hate the term *burglar*,' he said. 'It conjures up some sneak thief in the night. I usually stole from houses to which I was invited, and only the best jewellery from the best people. Whilst on the run, I thought it best to adopt a very different persona' (which means, 'I thought it was a good idea to seem a very different type of bloke.'). 'Do either of you have a knife?'

'What about the one you stuck in my back to keep me quiet?' Eddie demanded, still reeling at Barking's transformation.

'That was no knife, Eddie,' he said. 'It was a half-chewed carrot I found in your pocket when I put on your clothes.'

Eddie groaned. He'd been tricked by his own

whittling carrot! Skillet, meanwhile, cautiously handed Barking a pocket knife.

Barking lined up Eddie and the newcomers in front of the hole, so he could keep the gun trained on everybody. Crouching down, but without taking his eyes off anyone for a moment, he cut open one of the sandbags with the knife. And can you guess what poured out? Sand, of course – they were sandbags . . . but when Barking put his free hand into the sack, he pulled out a fistful of jewels.

True to form, the jewels glinted in the sunlight, just as all jewels should. He put in his hand again and pulled out more. There were necklaces, ear-rings, brooches, bracelets: gold, silver, diamonds, rubies, sapphires, pearls.

'How did they get into our sandbags?' gasped Skillet, Zucchini's props man, amazed that they'd been carrying around a fortune without even knowing it!

'The sandbags were made at the prison . . .' Eddie recalled. 'Zucchini said that they usually sewed mailbags but they'd sewn these sandbags specially for him –'

'Quiet, *please*!' commanded Barking. 'Mr Skillet. You look to me like a man who is good at knots.'

Several hours later, when the rector of St Botolph's was taking a short cut across the field to the church, he noticed someone had been digging near the churchyard wall.

'What a silly place to dig a hole!' he thought. 'Anyone might fall in!' When he peered inside he found the Great Zucchini, his manger Mr Merryweather, his props man Mr Skillet, his love-ly assistant Daniella, and a man with a huge walrus moustache all tied together with a single piece of rope. Each had a gag in his – or her – mouth, made from what appeared to be a torn-off strip of hessian sacking. They were sitting on an empty coffin and were speckled with sand.

Having helped to free them, the rector was later horrified to discover that all but one of them was, for one reason or another, wanted by the police!

But what of Eddie and Barking (as Arthur Brunt the billionaire burglar from Barking now chose to be called)? They were in a hearse, rattling at breakneck speed towards the moors, the tiny convict cracking the whip like a mad circus ring-master.

That Sinking Feeling

*In which most of Eddie's family cram themselves
into a basket*

Wolfe Tablet, the famous photographer – and there were very few photographers back then, famous or otherwise – stood in the police inspector's office, looking out of the window at his precious hot-air balloon.

'I'm very grateful that you retrieved my balloon, inspector,' he said, 'but what I fail to understand is why I cannot take it with me. I have a race meeting to attend. I intend to photograph the galloping horses from the air.'

'We need to keep it as evidence,' said Mr Chevy,

the peeler stationed at the door.

'Evidence,' said the inspector from behind his desk. Well, his loud-check-covered tummy was immediately behind his desk. The rest of him was up against the wall.

'But you have eyewitnesses who can swear in court who stole my balloon and it was your own men who got it back for me. Surely you don't need to keep it tethered here until the trial?' the photographer protested.

'The law's the law,' said the peeler.

'The law's the law,' said the inspector. If the truth be told, the police were desperate to hold on to something. Zucchini and his staff had escaped, taking the recently captured hearse with them. All the police had left in this whole case was the hot-air balloon, so they were more than a little reluctant to let it go. That and the fact that it was great fun to go up and down in when they had nothing better to do . . . which was why the envelope (the actual balloon part above the basket) was fired up and ready to fly. A bit of a giveaway!

'But the balloon is my livelihood!' Wolfe Tablet complained. He was an important man. An impressive man. A man used to having his own way. The inspector squirmed in his creaking chair.

At that moment, the door to the office burst open and in marched Mad Uncle Jack and Even

Madder Aunt Maud, holding Malcolm the stuffed stoat like a baby, closely followed by Mr and Mrs Dickens (still without her wedding ring).

'Is he here?' Mad Uncle Jack demanded.

'Is who where?' spluttered the inspector, struggling to his feet. 'What is the meaning of this intrusion?'

'My boy, Eddie Dickens. Have you locked him up again? He's gone missing,' said Mrs Dickens.

The inspector raised an eyebrow and looked across to Mr Chevy. The peeler shook his head. 'No, sir,' he said.

'No we haven't,' said the inspector, 'and the last time we locked him up he signed a piece of paper saying he didn't mind. Isn't that right, Mr Chevy?'

'Indeed it is, inspector,' agreed the peeler. 'He signed along the dotted line. I drew the dots myself.'

'It's not then we're worried about,' said Mad Uncle Jack. 'It's last night. He didn't sleep in his bed.'

'Well, his bed was blown up a few days ago,' Mad Aunt Maud explained, instantly making matters more complicated, 'but he wasn't in the bed he should have been sleeping in since his bed was blown up, if you see what I mean?'

The inspector obviously didn't.

'What matters is that my son is missing!' Mrs Dickens wailed.

'And Malcolm wasn't trying to poison me at all,' said Mad Aunt Maud. 'That was a misunderstanding. It wasn't a poison pill, but a wedding ring. It bounced right off his nose, you see?'

'Malcolm? Who's Malcolm? And what's all this about exploding beds and poison pills that aren't poison pills . . .?'

'My wife is a little confused,' said Mad Uncle Jack, in a whisper loud enough to wake the police-station cat, which had been sleeping under the inspector's desk. 'She is, of course, referring to Sally, who is stuffed.'

'I'd like to report my son missing,' said Mr Dickens, who hadn't heard a word. 'His name is Edmund Dickens.'

'Sometimes known as Eddie?' asked a smallish man, stepping through the open doorway. He wore a pinstripe suit, speckled with sand. Nobody saw his lips move because they were covered by a large walrus moustache.

'And who are you, sir?' sighed the inspector.

'He's the librarian –'

'The gas man –'

'The dog-catcher –'

'The tree-counter –'

You see, our Mr Lalligag had given himself a different cover story – a different identity – to just about everyone he'd met at Awful End. Now he

120

spoke the truth. 'My name is Abe Lalligag from the Pickleton Detective Agency and I am on the trail of some missing jewels, stolen by Arthur Brunt the billionaire burglar.'

'From Barking?' asked the inspector. 'He's one of the convicts who escaped from Grimpen Jail.'

'And, I'm afraid he has taken Eddie Dickens hostage,' said the detective. 'I too was held prisoner until half an hour ago. I was rescued by a passing rector. There's no time to lose. We must save the boy and reclaim the jewels!'

'A passing what?' asked Mr Dickens.

'Rector!' said Mrs Dickens.

'Where do you think he's taken the boy?' asked the inspector.

'To the moors!' said the detective. 'In a hearse.' He caught sight of Wolfe Tablet's balloon through the window. 'That would be an ideal mode of transport. Come on!'

Before the inspector or his loud-checked suit had time to protest, everyone piled out of his office, down the corridor and out to the balloon.

Beating off the competition with her stuffed stoat, Mad Aunt Maud was the first into the basket, with a leg up from Mad Uncle Jack, who stepped in with ease after her. Mr Lalligag of the Pickleton Detective Agency was next on board and he was already untying the guy ropes as Mr and Mrs Dickens scrambled in after him.

The balloon basket was already off the ground as Wolfe Tablet made it aboard his own contrivance, but the police inspector and Mr Chevy the peeler were far too slow.

No matter how much they stood on the ground, shaking their fists and crying 'Come back!' the balloon was up, up and away on its rescue mission.

'How do you make this thing go left or right?' demanded Detective Lalligag. 'Is there some kind of lever?'

'Air currents!' said Wolfe Tablet, adjusting the flame in the burner under the hole in the middle of the balloon envelope, so that it made the air inside it hotter and so rise. (Hot air rises. Even hotter air rises even higher. So now you know.)

'We fly up until we find the air currents – winds – in the direction we want to go.'

'Which is over there!' Mr Lalligag pointed.

Mr Tablet was a skilled balloonist and it wasn't long before he had them flying over the moors.

'There!' cried Mad Uncle Jack, leaning right out of the basket and pointing.

'What is it?' asked Mad Aunt Maud.

'A gorse bush the colour of my favourite old waistcoat.'

'Oh, so it is! Look, Malcolm!' She held the stuffed stoat, nose first, over the side.

'Any sign of my poor Eddie?' Mrs Dickens wailed.

'Not yet, madam . . . but look! There's the hearse!'

Sure enough, there below them – looking no larger than two gerbils pulling a shoe box – were the black horses and the hearse, abandoned by Barking as he and Eddie had carried on by foot.

'Look!' cried Aunt Maud excitedly, and everyone piled over to her side of the basket. 'That stream looks like a wiggly blue snake from up here!'

'It is the boy and the convict we're after!' Mr Lalligag fumed. 'The boy and the convict!'

Meanwhile, Mr Tablet had opened a wooden box fixed to one of the sides of the basket and was putting together a piece of complicated photographic equipment which he called a camera.

'Photographs of the capturing of the billionaire burglar would be a sensation!' he declared.

'We've got to find him first . . . There!' said the detective triumphantly. 'That's them!' And, sure enough, it was. There below was Barking with Eddie close behind, running through a patch of ferns almost as tall as they were. Eddie was carrying a carpet bag and, by the way he was struggling, Mr Lalligag reasoned that it must contain the stolen jewels. 'Can you bring this balloon down ahead of them?' he asked.

'It might be a bit of a bump, but I can indeed,' said Wolfe Tablet. He fiddled with the burner, pulled a rope or two and they were soon going down all right!

'Wheeeeeee!' said Mad Aunt Maud. 'We're flying, Malcolm. Flying!'

If Daniella's landing in the rose bed at Awful End had been undignified, this landing was a total disgrace! Of all the places they could have landed, they hit a rocky outcrop on a slope and the basket tipped over, with everyone still inside it, and then the balloon dragged them along the ground. There were plenty of 'oohs!', 'arghs!' and 'oofs!' and each and every one of them who'd been through the experience now knew what it felt like to be one of a litter of unwanted kittens inside an old coal sack stuffed with rocks.

Wolfe Tablet clutched his beloved wooden box camera to protect it as best he could. Mad Aunt Maud hugged Malcolm and Mad Uncle Jack hugged her. Detective Lalligag and Mr Dickens held on to each other, and Mrs Dickens held on to the edge of the basket.

They'd all managed to get about as upright as they could when Barking came running out of the patch of ferns. The last thing on earth he'd expected was this extraordinary welcoming committee, and he came to a halt.

'Give it up, Brunt,' said Mr Lalligag. 'You're a gentleman burglar, not a violent man. You're outnumbered and would have to shoot us all in order to escape.'

Barking glared back at him. 'We meet again, Lalligag!' he said, because that's the kind of thing criminal masterminds always seem to say when finally face to face with the detective who's been tracking them down. 'I'm not going back to the stinking jail and I'm not giving up my treasure after all this time!' He looked furious. *Fuming*.

'Er, why are you wearing my son's clothes?' asked Mr Dickens, stepping forward. Lalligag put out a hand to stop him. Eddie's father, still being deaf from the blast, really had little if any idea who was what or what was going on.

Barking put his hand on the butt of the

125

revolver tucked into the waistband of his – yes, all right, *Eddie's* – trousers. 'I have a simple proposition,' he said.

Eddie found it hard to believe that this was the same man who'd been sniffing thistles and licking ears . . . or perhaps the ear-licking had really been instruction-whispering, all a part of Barking's – of Brunt's – pretence.

'If I let the boy go unharmed, then you, in return, must let me go with the jewels,' said Barking. 'If you follow me, however, I shall start shooting. I can't say fairer than that.'

Lalligag appeared to be considering the proposition, when a couple of newcomers arrived on the scene.

'First, tell me this,' said a voice from the top of a nearby hummock – or was it a hillock? (I always have this problem.) Everyone turned to look.

'Ah, the local ironmonger!' cried Mad Uncle Jack.

'Hello, Mr Collins,' Even Madder Aunt Maud waved. 'Coooeee! I've been racking my brains and I've remembered that I *do* like you!'

It was, if the truth be told, the Great Zucchini. He was riding a 'borrowed' carthorse bareback, with the lovely Daniella up behind him, frilly petticoats rustling in the breeze. 'How did your stolen jewels come to be in my sandbags?' he demanded.

'Daniella!' cried Eddie, dropping the carpet bag. 'You came to rescue me!'

'It was Harold's idea,' she called down. 'He didn't want to leave you with the likes of 'im!'

The likes of 'im – that is to say, Barking, or Arthur Brunt the billionaire burglar, if you prefer – pulled himself to his full (if somewhat small) height and looked across to the escapologist on horseback, but kept his hand firmly gripped around the revolver. Then a look of smug pride shaped his features.

'When I was tried, convicted and sent to jail, they never found the latest batch of jewels I'd stolen. They searched my house, my hideout and dug up half of Barking, but never recovered a single sparkler.' (No, he wasn't talking about fireworks. A sparkler is slang for a gem or diamond.) 'They never found them because I'd smuggled them into jail with me. And who'd think of looking for them there? When I, along with Bonecrusher, Swags and the others found a way to escape, I didn't want to risk being captured with the jewels . . . so when you came to the jail requesting we sew sandbags for your act, I came up with the plan to fill them with my ill-gotten gains –'

'So the stolen jewels "escaped" first, then you followed and came to get them back!' said Eddie.

'Exactly . . .'

'Why all the talking?' demanded Mr Dickens, who'd seen a lot of mouth-opening and closing, but hadn't heard an actual word that was said. 'We're only a few pages from the end of the final episode. What we need is *action*, not words!' Of course, no one had any idea what he meant, but his words did have some surprising results.

'One thing you should know, Brunt,' cried Lalligag, lowering his head and charging across the springy moorland grass like an angry bull in a bullfight, 'is that I never load my gun!'

Startled, Barking pulled out the revolver he'd taken off Lalligag earlier, and – to his credit, I suppose – fired it up in the air rather than straight at the oncoming detective, just in case the Pickleton detective was lying and it was loaded.

There was a resounding 'CLICK'.

Lalligag wasn't lying: the gun was empty.

Barking dodged the detective, grabbed the bag from Eddie, who was too startled by the speed of the snatch to put up much of a struggle, and darted off down the hillside.

The Great Zucchini and Daniella came thundering down off the tummock – that's it: it was neither a hummock nor a hillock – on the carthorse, galloping after him. Mad Uncle Jack, Even Madder Aunt Maud and Eddie's parents were also in hot pursuit, with Eddie close behind.

Only Wolfe Tablet stood his ground, because he was setting up a tripod and taking pictures.

'Nobody steals my great-nephew's clothes and gets away with it!' cried Mad Aunt Maud, who wasn't particularly clear about the escaped-convicts/stolen-jewels/escapologist side of things, but was fully aware that Eddie shouldn't be walking around the misty moors in next to nothing . . . and she dived onto the ground, throwing out her arms to catch the iron ball that Barking was now dragging behind him.

To us, it would have looked like something out of a game of rugby, but – although it was first played in the 1820s – no one had come up with any proper rules yet, so few people had been to a rugby match.

It didn't stop Barking, though. He just kept on running across the springing turf, with Mad Aunt Maud being dragged behind.

When she'd made that dramatic dive, Malcolm – or is it Sally? – had flown out of her hands and been caught brilliantly by Eddie, running alongside.

He was bursting with pride that his great-aunt had taken such direct action against a master criminal, and was inspired to act himself. He threw Malcolm as hard as he could towards the fleeing convict.

There was a loud 'THUD' of stuffed stoat coming into contact with back of human head, followed by a cry. Barking stopped running, but the carpet bag kept on going: it flew out of his tiny paws and burst open, its glittering contents spilling onto the ground . . .

. . . and what dangerous ground! Without even realising it at first, Eddie had just saved Barking's life, possibly a number of their lives. They'd been heading straight for the bog!

At first glance, the land just ahead of them looked as solid as the ground surrounding it, with tufts of grass and heather sprouting up, covering its dangerous secret. Just beneath the surface was mud deep enough to suck down a herd of wild deer – and certainly a tiny convict weighed down with a ball and chain – never to be seen again.

'Good shot!' cried Daniella.

'My jewels!' cried Barking, watching them sink without trace for ever. 'No!' And the cry transformed into the plaintive cry of a howling hound: 'Oooo-ooooooooooow!'

Eddie thought back to the night in the cave and wondered if there really was more of a doggy side to Arthur Brunt than the billionaire burglar himself realised.

'Well done, Malcolm!' said Mad Aunt Maud, struggling to her feet and retrieving her beloved stoat. She held him by the tail and brought him down on Barking's head for good measure.

'You're a naughty, naughty man!' she told him.

Mr Lalligag of the Pickleton Detective Agency stepped forward and handcuffed the defeated villain. He'd lost the jewels but got his man.

Eddie looked around him. He hadn't felt so happy in ages. His family had come to rescue him . . . even Daniella and the Great Zucchini had come to his aid. And it was he, Eddie – with a little help from a stuffed stoat who was as good as family – who had finally stopped Barking. He wanted to remember this moment for ever. Fortunately, someone else had the same bright idea.

'Everyone smile, please!' said Wolfe Tablet. 'And don't move!'

There was a bright flash and a loud bang, followed by a smell of sulphur.

And that, once again, dear readers, is the end of another of Eddie Dickens's rather strange adventures. For those of you who don't like questions left unanswered and loose ends untied, let me try to put your minds at rest.

I should start by telling you that Wolfe Tablet was so pleased to have been in on the capture of the billionaire burglar that he eventually dropped all charges against Zucchini's troupe for tying him up in the Rancid Rat and stealing his precious hot-air balloon. The original photograph of Eddie next to the handcuffed Barking can still be seen in the Wolfe Tablet Museum in the West Country. (I forget where it is exactly, and I don't have my guide book with me today. I've been there, though, and they do very good cream teas.)

Eddie's father's hearing returned completely, eventually, and Mad Aunt Maud's injuries – from being hit by a balloon, dragged along in a balloon basket and pulled along the ground by a convict, whilst clutching his ball and chain – soon healed. Mad Uncle Jack bought a new waistcoat the colour of the gorse bush.

Malcolm was, I am pleased to report, undamaged by the part he played in the convict's heroic capture.

Eddie's mum, meanwhile, got her wedding ring back, but please don't ask me to go into details as to how.

The Great Zucchini and his escapology troupe moved on to tour the rest of the country, but not before a huge party was held at Awful End. Eddie found that he could speak to the lovely Daniella without dribbling and that girls are really just human beings after all.

Bonecrusher and the other escaped convicts were finally caught – all except for Swags, who somehow got away. Those of you who read the third and final book in this trilogy will run into him again . . . just as Eddie himself did.

Which leaves one final matter: that of the carthorse 'borrowed' by the Great Zucchini and Daniella when riding to Eddie's rescue. His owner eventually found him, chewing the plants in the rector of St Botolph's garden. You wouldn't know the man. Why should you? He was the local iron-monger. His name was Mr Collins.

THE END
until the next time

If you'd like to write to the author of
Dreadful Acts to tell him what you enjoy most
about Eddie Dickens's adventures, or to ask him
anything about the story or its characters, your
letters should be addressed to:

Philip Ardagh
c/o Faber and Faber
3 Queen Square
London
WC1N 3AU

If he's not too busy trying to untangle his
unruly beard or writing even more books,
he will send you a reply
(so don't forget to include your own address)
. . . but do be patient!